I0599988

Light Roast Larceny

A Coastal Coffee Mystery

Kate Montgomery

Magnolias Manuscripts Press

Copyright © 2025 by Kate Montgomery

All rights reserved.

No part of this publication may be reproduced, distributed, or transmitted in any form or by any means, including photocopying, recording, or other electronic or mechanical methods, without the prior written permission of the publisher, except as permitted by U.S. copyright law. For permission requests, contact Kate Montgomery.

The story, all names, characters, and incidents portrayed in this production are fictitious. No identification with actual persons (living or deceased), places, buildings, and products is intended or should be inferred. No AI was used in the creation of this work.

Book Cover by Ki Charm Kim

To those who make me feel like I can do this. Forever grateful.

Contents

Chapter One

Disturbing the Peace

I jolt awake with a gasp. Was that Brad's truck starting?

Catching my breath, I lay still in the early morning silence, straining to listen. No, not his truck. Reaching over I pat his side of the bed, seeking the warmth of his sleeping body. Instead, I feel the cool, crisp sheets.

Another morning that I've missed him leaving.

Yawning to the point my jaw nearly unhinges; I try to untangle myself and roll onto my side to look at the clock. Sure enough, it is after eight o'clock. Yet again, I've managed to sleep through both of our alarms. Bless him for getting up and getting out the door. Guess it's my turn. Groaning again, I scrunch up my pillow and grab my phone. Time to see what the day holds. Oh yeah- a whole lot of nothing. Not even worth it to open my calendar app. I used to live by what was on the calendar. These days, I have to find things to fill my time instead of having it filled by others.

I get to lay in bed and think about profound things like- why does getting up take a little bit longer each morning? I swear, the closer I get to forty, the longer it takes. In my teens and twenties, I'd pop up like a slice of toast, hit the shower and be out the door in under ten minutes. Not so much anymore. It is now an involved process. Stretching, grunting, slowly changing positions commences. Ultimately leading to me sitting on the edge of the bed.

Coffee is what gets me out of bed most mornings. That and tiny dogs barking to be let outside. Today will be no different. The coffee calls me like an ancient siren.

Nearly fifteen minutes later, I'm up. Coffee acquired, robe on, porch ready. Our dogs, Coco and Aggie (Chanel and Christie of course), eagerly follow me out into the warm morning sun. It isn't hot yet, but it will be soon enough. This morning routine has settled on me easily and we now look forward to it. A month ago, I wouldn't have thought so. I've learned to enjoy peace and quiet in the mornings.

Having always been more than a little nibby, getting to sit and watch my neighbors from the porch is right up my alley. The dogs love watching all the neighbors too. We hide out on the lanai and spy on the goings on. Despite living in a community filled with retirees, there is always something going on. It may sound boring to most, but we live for it.

Gliding into the day feels like a luxury. One I've not had for a VERY long time.

You see, three months ago, I would have already been sitting in my cube or rushing into the first meeting of the day. The ninety-minute, white-knuckle commute added to the daily adventure. Traffic into Miami gets interesting in the mornings. Not in a fun way either. More in an "am I getting an ulcer?" kind of interesting. Don't get me wrong- I thought I was living the dream. Until one day I wasn't. My routine crashed to the ground, shattering into a thousand pieces.

That was a moment frozen in time. It was an average Wednesday, sitting in my cube, fixing yet another presentation for a colleague when I got a message that my boss needed me ASAP. I assumed it was for our upcoming meetings with clients the next day. Nope! I was one of the lucky dozen or so getting laid off. Effective immediately, in a "grab your bag and potted plant, security is waiting for you" style.

Before you get too sad for me, it was actually okay. I got a more than generous severance. Benefits were covered by my husband, Brad, and we lead a normal lifestyle (i.e. live within our means or is that not normal?). Basically, it wasn't the worst thing to happen to me. I mean yeah- I bawled like a baby for a full day and had more wine than I should have at dinner that night. Then I realized, I didn't even like that job. In fact, I hated working there. A healthy dose of perspective (thanks babe!) and I came to the conclusion, that this might be my shot to figure out the burning question- what do I really want to do? Time for some in-depth soul searching.

I'm still going through my teenage list- florist, marine biologist, dog walker. The list goes on and on. The funny thing is, I never really decided what I wanted to be when I grew up. A generic degree in Business and Marketing was my major. I simply fell into my job, hopped one thing into the other, and there I landed. Initially, it seemed to be exactly what I was looking for. There were more opportunities to use my degree than other jobs in the past. But over time, it began to shift and it began to feel mundane. Who doesn't dream of building presentation decks and finding the perfect graphic? I cannot claim it was a passion, referring to it as a (seemingly) safe path is a better description. Which obviously backfired.

The looming question remains: What *do* I want to do? At the moment, drinking coffee in the sun sounds right. My future can be figured out later after I am properly caffeinated.

I'm stretched out on the chaise lounge, Coco under my knees and Aggie tucked under one arm. My coffee is empty and we're too cozy for me to consider getting up. A stack of books on the side table beckons me. I turn and start combing through. Reading is my favorite hobby, and I gobble up books by the dozens. Mysteries are the best. Especially if I can't figure out who did it. Finalizing my choice- a thriller set in an abandoned logging town, I lean back in my chair to read for a while.

"Hellllloooooo neighbor!" rings out loudly, echoing across the lawn. It's a shrill, nasal voice.

Edna has spotted me. The dogs go bananas, spinning in circles, yipping, and barking. It's an understatement to say, they're not huge fans of hers. Must have picked that up from me-don't they say dogs take after their owners?

"Hang on one sec, Edna!" I reluctantly call, then usher the dogs into the house. Pausing before turning around, I make sure my robe is secure. Flashing my 80-year-old, gossipy neighbor is not on the to-do list this morning. All put together with a fake smile slapped on my face. I return to the porch, turning in time to see Edna at the edge of the walk. She moves quickly for an octogenarian in need of a hip replacement.

"No job yet, huh?" Edna begins directly. She's known for her heat-seeking conversation techniques. My brain begins flashing warning signals. Oh God, she's showing no mercy this morning.

"Well, I'm taking it slow. I've been enjoying a little bit of a break," I coolly snap back, immediately offended. My cheeks warm, and I can feel the flush spreading. A scowl replaces my smile. I am trying to keep my cool, but it is way too early for this. I'm not nearly caffeinated enough for a verbal sparring match.

Edna huffs loudly and says, "I'd think you'd want to get right back to it, with the way you all are these days."

Um, no idea what that is supposed to mean. So, I will proceed lightly. "We decided that it is okay for me to take the time at home for now."

"Oh, how nice *dear*. Perhaps you can use that time to work on the house," she runs her eyes over the front of our house and down the side. The "dear" seems as disingenuous as a "bless your heart" would have. Edna's brow is furrowed, her arms are crossed. Disapproval written boldly across her face.

Again, yikes. I don't know what to do with that. "It will be nice to have some free time. There's always a to-do list. Well Edna, as usual, it's been a delight, but I've got to get crackin' on that list."

Sensing she's getting the brush off, Edna tenses but wraps up the conversation with a terse, "I'll see you soon," and heads home. Again, moving with deceptive speed. At the end of my walk, she points at the base of my tree, indicating the wreath of weeds. With an obnoxious finger wave, she finally walks down the street. I briefly consider sending out a text to let our other neighbors know she's out and about. A quick pat down before I realize, I have no idea where my phone is.

I do love our little neighborhood for the most part but geez. There are moments when I wish we had a little more space or privacy. How would I describe it other than boundaries? The kind that doesn't require a fence line. I'm sure Edna will find a way to tattle on me to my husband when he gets home. This is a pattern. We always have a neighbor that tattles on me for something or another. Anyhow, better go hide in the house or pretend to work on a nonexistent to-do list.

Chapter Two

Errands and Incidents

F lash forwards a few hours to me reading on the couch. To my credit, at least I was reading instead of watching pointless videos on my phone again. I'll gladly take the win. A benefit to being home is my to-be-read pile has moved to a books-I've-read pile. Hours pass quickly as I devour book after book. I've fallen into a new mystery series and cannot get enough. Solving the mystery before the book gives up the details is a highlight for me and I take a ridiculous amount of pride in it. This book has me stumped and I am loving it.

Sadly, it is time to head into town to grab stuff for dinner. Yet again, I failed to plan and therefore I plan to fail. Reluctantly I close my book and shuffle into the kitchen. Staring into the fridge leads to no inspiration. Which is anticipated, I'm not good on the fly. Collapsing onto a bar stool, I text my sister, Cassi, for input.

Me- *help!! No plans for dinner*

Cassi- *Grill?* with a shrug emoji

Me- *lame*

Cassi- *happy to help*

Not exactly the level of assistance I'd hoped for. But I can work with that. Grilling is usually in my skillset. She's well aware of abilities, or lack thereof. The question still remains- grill what? That is yet to be determined, I could add a salad, baked potatoes, and wine on the back deck. Sounds perfect, right?

I am blessed with the most relaxed husband. He will be down for whatever, as usual. Thanking my lucky stars for his chill. I swear he has no preference for dinner- whatever it is, he eats it.

Killing additional time, I debate taking my bike the few miles to the store. Picturing myself damp and smelly makes driving an easier decision. Plus, being in my car makes me happy. It is the cutest thing ever. For years, I had driven the typical comfortable commuter sedan. But two years ago, as an anniversary gift, my husband bought my dream car. Since we moved closer to the beach, he said I needed my beach vehicle. Cute and compact, my soft-top red Jeep is a bright spot. Definitely did not fit in at the work garage but sure does in here. Another sign that it was more than time to move on.

Sliding into the driver's seat, I throw a handful of shopping totes in the passenger seat and run through a quick double-check for my wallet (my most commonly forgotten item) before leaving. While backing out of our short driveway, I spot Edna chatting with her little group on the corner. None of the four make any attempt not to stare.

Wait. Is Edna actually pointing at the side of my house?

Come on, now. The side yard needs a little refresh, but it isn't bad. Or maybe it is. Time to view through the nosey neighbor lenses, I guess. Adding that to my ever-growing list, the real one. I slip my sunglasses down into place and drive past with my head held high.

Driving through our neighborhood, my mood boosts, and I sigh happily. Brad and I both grew up in northern Florida and dreamt of living farther south. After college, each of our moves pushed us down the state little by little. Every time in a rental a little nicer than the last. This is our first home that we've owned. Five years ago, the tight vintage neighborhood with the odd name felt like paradise. The cadre of elderly neighbors welcomed us with open arms and baked goods by the dozens. It felt like we'd moved into the set of a sitcom. As some of those original neighbors have passed on or moved into care homes, new and less friendly versions have replaced them. The vibe of the place shifted. A tight community feels like tight jeans now.

Despite all the changes, the single-story bungalows on narrow lots continue to delight me. Banana trees and palms are in heavy rotation. It is peak Florida-cutesy. Each time I pull in the drive and see our community sign, it makes me happy. I wouldn't give it an award for creativity but certainly would for how precious it is. A large white wooden sign, with a massive flamingo painted a tropical mint, the community's name, *Mint Flamingo Bungalows,* in bubble-gum pink painted below is a remarkable sight. Spotlights at night light it up and the colors seem to glow. There's no way to miss the entrance of our neighborhood.

Tourists will occasionally pull their cars over to take photos with the sign. Every time it pops up on social media, our out-of-town friends and family tag us. They find it hilarious the joy the sign brings to the public. In fairness, I get about as much joy as the tourists. I've taken about fifty selfies with it over the years. When Brad was out of town on a work trip last year, the dogs and I sent him photos every evening with it. Giggling to myself, I think of the photos I've seen him sneak, despite his claims of it being tacky.

Moving on, back to the tasks at hand. Groceries. Another thing I have noticed in the last few weeks, I can get WAY off track, in a heartbeat. Zero to down the rabbit hole. Dinner is my priority currently, once I get it handled, then I'll think about the other lists circling in my head. Decision made, I am refusing to let joblessness and biddies drag me down! It is a path that I can't sacrifice the time to go down.

Music blasting, sun shining, wind in my hair, I turn onto the main road. Palm trees and brightly colored buildings blur past me as I pick up speed. Could today be more perfect? This is also why we chose south Florida. The sunshine and warmth revive us. My husband tells me I'm like a lizard, I need all the heat! Terrarium is my preferred temperature and humidity level.

Driving with the top down, the sun perks me up in no time. I feel my skin tingle beneath its heat. As I savor the temperature, I make a mental note to grab more sunscreen at the store.

Fighting the trapped shopping carts, I finally struggle through freeing one and begin meandering the aisles. Despite my relaxing drive over, I haven't come up with any solid ideas for dinner. My meal inspiration resembles a black hole. Scrolling the internet didn't help either, maybe looking at random foods or sale items will inspire me. I begin tossing items at random into the cart. No actual meal is coming together, instead the cart is filling with pre-made foods, snacks, and sweets. By the looks of it, I am feeding hungry teenagers not two 30-somethings on a budget. Stopping to survey the disturbing collection in my cart, I pull out my phone to text my sister again or maybe my aunt. One of them will have a suggestion.

Mid-way into my texts, I hear a pleasant warbling, "It's my lovely Cici," from the end of the aisle.

There's only one person who calls me, her "lovely Cici." My neighbor two doors down, Mirabel Hernandez. A precious ninety-three-year-old widow who moved from Cuba in her early twenties as a newlywed. She's walking the line between independence and frailty. I adore her. At the sound of her greeting, I spin my cart to rush toward her. She is all smiles and peers at me through the thick lenses of her lime green glasses. Today, they match her outfit, often they do not. And she couldn't care less either way. She is not quite five feet tall and nearly level with the items piled high in her cart. I am in awe of how she's able to navigate through the store.

"Mrs. H! How are you pushing all that around?" I ask on my approach, dramatically going up on tiptoes.

"Alfie is here, don't worry," she responds with a chuckle. My face must have given my inner monologue away. Alfie is her son who has recently retired and visits weekly. "We are getting ready for a family dinner."

"Huh! I should have called you before I came and tried to figure out dinner here at the store," I say while waving at the mismatched hoard of groceries in my cart.

Without further prompting, she gives me a few dinner ideas. All of which, I quickly note in my phone. I have struck meal-planning gold. This woman is a life saver! Alfie joins her side from another aisle, and we chat for another few minutes. I bid them well wishes on their upcoming dinner and take off to buy items with an actual plan.

Armed with a list, I make a beeline for the meat counter. I put in an order for a mountain of meat. Turning to check my list, a cart gently taps into the side of mine. Startled, I glance up quickly and meet the gaze of Desmond Canistel, a feisty gentleman who also lives in my neighborhood. He is quite the joker and always up for a prank or a trick. It is one of the things I appreciate most about him. Aging has not diminished his love of mischief, and I hope it never does.

Recently, his wife of sixty-three years, Karen, had to go into a nursing home. He's been lonely ever since. Going to the community center and the store gets him out of the house. I see him at Bingo every time I volunteer. He shows up early and offers to stay after for clean-up, maximizing the time he spends with us.

"What's for supper neighbor? If it sounds good enough, I might invite myself over," he says as a greeting, a twinkle in his eye.

"Thanks to Mrs. Hernandez, I've at least got a plan. Can't vouch for the taste though." I am not known for my skills in the kitchen. Many of our neighbors have been tortured with my baked goods. He knows it is best to avoid untested recipes.

While waiting for my order, we catch up on life and how Karen is doing. I am happy to hear she's doing well and has adjusted to her new routine. The stroke had come out of nowhere and was devastating for both of them. Karen was fiercely independent. A woman in charge, who took care of their lives, making it all look effortless. When she was hospitalized, it was sudden and shocking. Learning she wouldn't be able to return home for a long time, if ever, was earth shattering. Knowing that both are adapting to new routines and she's making progress is fantastic news. We keep pulling for them, hoping and praying that Karen will improve enough to come home. Desmond asks about Brad and my job hunt, if there are any updates. I share that for now, I am content to be home and volunteer at the community center. I find it funny that Desmond asking doesn't upset me. Edna's inquiries instill a gut churning rage.

We part ways when he gives his order. I pop my ear buds in and head to the checkout. For once, I am looking forward to attempting dinner.

Unloading the bags of groceries from cart to car, I sing along to my Jimmy Buffet playlist. Parking my cart in the corral, I spy another neighbor in the lot. She's newer to our neighborhood, so I don't know her name yet. But we recognize each other. I take this as a chance to introduce myself properly. I call out a "hello" and walk toward her, waving pleasantly.

"Hi there! I'm Graciella Larkin, most everyone calls me Cici. My husband Brad and I live across from you. I've been meaning to introduce myself," a blush creeps up my neck and onto my cheeks. I feel like a bad neighbor for not making more of an effort.

"It's so nice to meet you! I've seen you around and have wanted to stop over to say hello. I'm Francine, Francine Cohen, my husband is Moshe. We moved here from Philadelphia," smiling, she admits, "Finally pulled the trigger after visiting for decades."

"Welcome!" I trill, my voice high and loud with enthusiasm. In an effort to avoid scaring her, I continue more conversationally, "We're so glad to have you. I'd offer to bake you some cookies, but I am awful at it. I can make a killer key lime pie though."

"I'll take you up on it! You're welcome to stop by anytime, I love having company."

We continue to talk about the community and activities that she and her husband may enjoy. I make a few recommendations for restaurants close to the neighborhood. Throughout our chat, a young man in a black t-shirt and jeans walks near us. Despite his well-kempt clothing, his ball cap and sunglasses give him a sketchy appearance, as if he's hiding his face.

Out of the corner of my eye, I've seen him walk a few laps around the small lot. He brushes past Francine's partially unloaded cart and mumbles a barely audible "S'cuse me." It seems odd for him to be so close to us in the parking lot, but you never know. People are generally a little weird. My assumption is he'd dropped something and is looking for it. He moves along finally, walking toward the street without interacting again. Before we part, I give Francine my phone number, she promises to call me later this afternoon.

Groceries loaded up and a solid dinner plan in place, I hop in the Jeep. Smiling ear to ear, I think about my neighbors' power to turn the afternoon around. Pork chops, black beans, sweet plantains, rice, and grilled jalapenos with a tasty iced cold margarita awaits! This day has vastly improved since my run-in with Edna. Proof that you can't let one person ruin the whole thing. I throw my sunglasses on and turn the radio up as I roar out of the parking lot.

At the light, I see the young man from the lot. He turns his head to check both directions, before stepping into the crosswalk. Earlier, I'd thought he seemed a little shady. He's removed the hat, and now appears young, clean-cut and non-threatening. The light changes and I take off, giving him no further thought. Suddenly remembering that I didn't get the sunscreen.

Chapter Three

Neighbor in Need

D ancing while cooking is one of the finer things in life. The beans are simmering, rice is steaming, sides are prepped, and the pork chops are stewing in the pressure cooker. I did a test batch of margaritas and they're some of my best work, if I do say so. Brad will be home in less than an hour, which means my timing is right on schedule. I am in awe of my togetherness, a celebratory dance break with the dogs on the porch is in order.

I turn to grab the remote off the windowsill and turn up the music. Nineties pop blares from the speaker on the counter. My phone buzzes on the counter with a number I don't recognize. Any other time, I wouldn't answer but in a split second I recall giving my number to Francine earlier at the store. The dance party will need to wait a few.

"Hello. This is Francine Cohen," an anxious voice greets my overly chipper hello. Glad I answered.

"Hey Francine! I thought it might be you."

"You did, why?" she answers with a bite of caution. It strikes me as an unusual response. A zip of anxiety runs through me. She called me, right? Furtively, I glance at the screen to confirm it's an incoming call.

"Oh, well, I'd given you my number at the store a little while ago, but I didn't have yours," fumbling with my justification and now feeling profoundly awkward, like I'm some type of weirdo. The dogs are scratching at the door to be let in, and Aggie begins barking manically. I rush over to open the door, momentarily distracted. I realize the line has gone silent.

"Francine, is everything, okay?" The silence continues and I hold the phone away from my face to make sure it is still connected. She's still there. I give it another try, "Francine?"

"I can't seem to find my wallet and I thought maybe you could help me," she says tearfully, "When I got home and unloaded everything, I can't find it." She sniffles and takes in a shuddering breath. " I get a little forgetful sometimes, but I swear I had it when I left the store. Moshe has been through the car and all of the bags several times." Uncharacteristically, I wait to let her finish, there seems to be more to the story.

"Right before the store, I'd visited the bank and taken money out. The envelope of cash was tucked inside my wallet. Several hundred dollars. I can't believe I would have just left my wallet at the store or in the cart." She stops talking and I hear her blowing her nose.

"I'm so sorry! Of course I'll help. Let me think for a sec," I pause. Tapping my nails against the counter while I collect bits and pieces of memories. An annoying habit, I am aware, but it helps me picture the scene. Puffing out a breath, I begin aloud with what I can remember, "Okay, we had our carts parked side by side. I'd walked over from the next row. The rear passenger door was open." Clicking my tongue against my teeth, I keep describing what I recall, "your purse was sitting in the back of the cart, on top of a few bags. Do you remember if it was closed?"

"I don't. I usually put it in the front part to keep an eye but must have moved it because of the bread and eggs."

"Wait!" I exclaim, "The young man!" I hear Francine gasp through the line and whisper an "oh."

"Did he brush against your cart? Could he have bumped into your cart and knocked it out?" I rush on.

"I think…. he was near both our carts," she says haltingly, as if she's trying to recall where we were in the lot. Since she's new to the area, I'm sure it is challenging to picture somewhere you've only been a handful of times.

"Same here. It was so strange that he came so close to us. The lot was fairly empty, it made no sense for him to keep walking around and stop near our carts."

"Do you think he could have taken my wallet?" anxiety rising in her voice.

"It's a possibility. I don't like to judge people, but it seemed so odd how close he came to us and now your wallet is missing. Have you called the store?"

"I did and they haven't found my wallet. Should I call the police?"

"It honestly sounds like you should. If you need anything from me- call me right away. My memory is decent, and I can probably describe him if needed."

"Oh goodness," Francine dissolves into sobs. "My daughter is going to be upset with me. She's always afraid something like this is going to happen. She always says she doesn't want me driving or running errands alone anymore. This is only going to add fuel to that fire."

"I'm sure it's nerve-wracking but this wasn't your fault, Francine. You were potentially pick-pocketed at the grocery store," I reassure her. In an attempt to lessen her stress, I offer "Do you want me to come over while you make the call?"

"No, I can do it. I'll call you if they need anything," she seems to be somewhat calmer and is not actively crying, only sniffling softly.

I offer her more reassurance of my support before hanging up. Sheesh! The poor thing. Bad enough to have your wallet stolen, but then to be nervous to tell your family on top of that. I make the snap decision to bake her the promised key lime pie since my kitchen is already torn up. Why not add to the mess? I twirl around to face my disaster of a kitchen and start gathering supplies. I crank up the music and get to work.

Despite not being a good baker (or cook), I make a devastatingly delicious key lime pie. It is the one thing I know I can make that will actually be good. The rest is all kind of so-so. Not looking for a compliment here, I've got decades of feedback to prove it. I simply do not have the flair for it. Mirabel, Linda, and Karen have tried for the last five years. Not to mention all the years my own mother and aunts have attempted. Bless my husband for continuing to eat homecooked food. That man is a trooper! Either that or he has no tastebuds. The jury is still out on that one. Pressure cookers and a grill have been the best things to happen to his meals around here.

The pies are in the oven when Brad walks through the door. He greets me with a kiss, and a comment on how delicious everything smells. Did I not tell you he's a gem? While I run through the menu, I pour him a frosty margarita and steer him to the lanai. Watching him walk out the door in front of me, I still get goosebumps. An astounding 6'4" and built like a man on the cover of a romance novel. Sandy hair, tan skin, and hazel eyes. He makes my heart pound just like it did when I met him in our Freshman Social Studies class.

I'm so distracted staring that I stub my toe and nearly fall out the door. My margarita sloshes a little and he turns to look, concerned by my sudden clumsiness.

"How many of those have you had?" he teases me.

I stick my tongue out and then lick the Tajin from the rim of my glass, throwing him an overly exaggerated wink. There's no way I am fessing up to my test batches earlier.

Our dogs rush in from the yard the second they lay eyes on Brad and jump all over him, nearly flinging margarita everywhere. He's learned to be faster than they are and balances it out of their reach. Once they've settled, I return with my own drink and a plate of cheese and crackers to munch on while dinner finishes. I tell him about running into Francine and the subsequent call. I haven't heard back from her and am a little worried.

Brad talks me down from calling her right now. "They're probably eating dinner. Give her time to call the police, talk to her family, and relax a bit. This has obviously been a lot for her."

I know he's right; she seemed so rattled that I am struggling to put our conversation out of my mind. Granted, I do not know her so she could be easily upset by nature, this could be her normal response. Who knows how I'd handle being pickpocketed at the store? I could be a bundle of nerves and tears. Somehow, I doubt it, but you never know until you're going through it.

Brad polishes off his margarita and heads to shower before we eat. Using the unexpected quiet, I take the chance to write out what I can remember from the encounter at the store today. Picturing what my favorite lady-sleuths would do- I draw a quick picture of where we were standing and even count how many parking spaces (let's be real, I estimated) from the store to the cars. The young man who passed us, this gets a little fuzzier here. I wish I had focused on his face! He was shorter than Brad, slim built, in jeans, and a dark T-shirt, with a ball cap pulled low over his face. At the time I didn't think much of it, with all the bright sun, it made sense to cover his face. There was something about his shoes though. They stick out in my mind, yet the actual detail escapes me. So frustrating! Tapping my nails on the table, I drum out a melody while trying to remember. What would one of my favorite detectives do to jog their memory?

I'm lost in my "case notes" when I feel a hand on my shoulders. Brad kisses the top of my head and murmurs, "Smoke detector" into the top of my head with a chuckle. I absentmindedly squeeze his hand and smile, taking in his clean, fresh-from-the-shower scent, I inhale deeply. Then my brain seems to catch up.

"Huh?" I spin to face him. "What about the smoke detector?"

"I turned it off when I hopped out of the shower," he says taking a seat across from me. With a wink, he grabs one of the small crackers and a piece of cheese and tosses them into his mouth.

Shrieking a colorful phrase that makes me blush, I rush into the kitchen. Stubbing my toe again and spilling my watered-down margarita in the process. I smell burnt food as I cross the threshold. My first thought is, "Not my pies!" I can't wreck the one thing I do well, it will ruin my track record.

A quick kitchen survey commences. The pressure cooker has reached its time and appears to be fine. No smoke or alarms. Facing the stove, I see the pot of black beans. It has scorched to the pan and now resembles chunky roof tar. The scent is just as appealing. A tiny gag escapes as I take the pot to the sink. Hot water has got to help this situation somehow. When the puff of foul-smelling steam hits my face, it makes me question the wisdom of this decision.

Coughing the stench away, I remember the pies in the oven.

Tossing the ruined pan and its revolting contents into the sink, I yank the oven door open with a force that nearly pulls the handle off. A sigh of relief escapes followed by a whoop of excitement. Despite forgetting the timer and losing track of time, the pies are both cooked perfectly. Not even a trace of burned graham cracker crust. I grab a tea towel decorated with flamingos and orange blossoms and lift the first pie out and onto the stovetop. Success! One down, one to go.

Brad leans across our small kitchen island as I remove the second one. I'm careful to reposition the tea towel to avoid the damp spots. Having cleared the oven door, I spin with a flair to show him my beautiful pie. In the process, it slips from my towel covered hands. With a wet plopping sound, it lands in a heap on the counter in front of Brad. We stare in stunned silence for a few seconds.

I cover my mouth with the towel to lessen the volume of my shriek of horror. Once I've gotten it out of my system, Brad pops around the counter and grabs two spoons from the drawer. He scoops up some of the pie and gently samples it.

"Mmmmm...blistering but delicious," he mumbles around the mouthful of the hot pie filling. He scoops another bite and offers it to me, wiggling the spoon back and forth. I shrug and lean forward. We might as well sample it now, then we can trash it.

"Oh my God! That's the best one yet!" I exclaim. Despite the lava-esque temperature, the flavor is amazing. I scoop the remaining pie into a container and figure we can cobble together a dessert from it.

By some miracle, the rest of dinner was salvageable and shockingly delicious. Brad raves about the pork chops, asking about my inspiration. I unabashedly reveal my source, Mirabel.

"I thought maybe petty crime was the secret ingredient," a mischievous grin on his face.

I cackle, in a very un-ladylike fashion. Thankfully, we have a remarkably similar sense of humor. The remainder of dinner is spent trading quips on my cooking skills.

Chapter Four

A Friendship Begins

Every night after dinner, Coco and Aggie demand a walk around the cul-de-sac. Rain or shine, they need to walk. We have turned it into a family event, and now it is a part of our daily routine. Our neighbor across the street, Linda, a retired high school teacher, keeps dog biscuits by the front door and water on her porch. If she spots us coming, she'll come out to say hello and chat. I don't know what the dogs love more, the attention they get or the actual walk. Either way they have fun, charging through the street like a mini dogsled team. But instead of huskies, Coco is a Pomeranian mix, and Aggie is an itty-bitty Bichon. They still think they're mighty.

Mid-way through the walk, I hear my name. The voice is quiet enough that it is hard to pinpoint exactly where it is coming from. I turn to Brad and he shrugs. He's obviously heard it as well. On the third, harshly whispered, "Cici!" Brad pokes me in the ribs and points across the street.

Francine is frantically waving to us. She is camped out in the side yard, on a glider under a large palm. In the dim evening light, she's hardly visible. Brad glances at me with a raised eyebrow and I return it with a "heck if I know" expression of my own. He sighs and reaches for the dog leashes, I blow him an air kiss, and he turns toward our house.

"Be home before midnight Super Sleuth," he calls over his shoulder. Both dogs have spotted Linda in her front yard and are charging toward her yipping happily. Their near run is barely above a walk for my husband. I shake my head at their shenanigans and walk to the anxious Francine.

Francine pats the spot next to her on the rocker, and I take a seat. She's obviously been crying. Her face is puffy, her eyes and nose are red, and she's twisting a damp tissue in her hand. I debate if I should be the first to speak. Normally, I'd plunge right in. While I'm still thinking, Francine blows her nose loudly into the tissue and takes a shuddering breath. Taking this as a cue to stay quiet, I lean over and gently pat her forearm. This seems to be the right thing to do, she begins to calm and as we sit, her breathing steadies.

"Francine, is there something you'd like to talk about?" I ask after a few moments.

"I told my family, and it didn't go so well. My husband called my daughter and son-in-law. We had a 'family meeting' before calling the police. It was a nightmare. Tamara, that's my daughter, was frustrated that I'd lost *another* wallet. I tried to explain that I thought it had been stolen and even had a witness. But Moshe and I don't think she believed me," Francine pauses to wipe the tears away. They're running down her cheeks and dripping off her chin. She's clearly hurt by her daughter's reaction, and it is breaking my heart. This poor sweet woman.

"My memory can be spotty. I don't know if you know that. Tamara thinks I've simply lost my wallet. I got so flustered trying to explain meeting you and the man in the lot. I had an even harder time. I couldn't tell her your name or many of the details. Mostly, I cried," she holds a hand to her reddened cheek, obviously embarrassed to be telling me this. "Tamara is insistent on making me an appointment with a neurologist. She wants me to get checked for Alzheimer's. By the time we finished the call, I was so upset that I couldn't speak. Moshe had to call the police. Of course, they didn't believe me either," she tips her head down into her hands and sobs quietly. Without thinking, I throw my arm around Francine, and she leans into me heavily while she cries, her body sagging into dead weight.

"Oh Francine! How can I help? Would you like me to talk with your family? Or go to the police with you? Whatever you need- I'm here for you," I reassure her, patting her back in what I hope is a soothing gesture. She continues to cry quietly without answering. The day seems to have been too much for her. Just like Brad had said it would be. Doggone him for being right again. Her memory must be giving her problems if she doesn't recall telling me about her forgetfulness earlier in the day. What will be the best way for me to help her?

A stern *ahem* from behind us interrupts my musings. To avoid tipping Francine over, I crane my neck over her head awkwardly. The man standing about a foot away does not appear to be pleased. A deep frown creases his forehead, his mouth is turned down, and his cheeks are faintly reddened. He seems almost angry to find me sitting with Francine. When I make eye contact, he advances forward. Uh-oh. I suddenly wish Brad had stayed.

"You must be Moshe. I'm Cici," I say in an overly cheery voice that feels completely inappropriate for the situation. Attempting a half-hearted wave with my free hand, I think *be pleasant*. I can feel my chest beginning to tighten and my breathing changes. Suddenly there seems to be a shortage of fresh air.

Francine sits upright and with a final sniffle says, "Calm down Moshe, I invited her."

Like a bull diverted from a charge, he changes his path and takes a seat in a chair opposite us. His face relaxes, although it remains reddened. I breathe a tiny sigh of relief, still with a twinge of tightness in my chest. Moshe is a big man and is intimidating when making a beeline for you. An easy smile has replaced the frown. Stretching forward, he extends his hand to make a proper introduction.

"I'm Moshe Cohen. You must be the lovely young woman who must have helped my Francy this afternoon."

"That's me! It's a pleasure to meet you. Cici Larkin, my husband Brad and I live right over there," I gesture to our house down the block. Brad is walking up our front steps with the dogs. In a moment of perfect timing, he turns as I point and wave. He returns the wave with a puzzled but pleasant expression. Bless his friendliness.

"It seems I interrupted a chat you were having," Moshe begins slowly.

"I was telling Cici how it went this evening," a sniffling Francine replies. Moshe's face transforms again. He doesn't look angry, he looks sad this time.

"When we told Tamara, it didn't go exactly how Francy or I had hoped it would. She got wound up. As usual," he says grimacing. Sharing family business does not seem to be in his comfort zone. "Not being able to recall your name on the spot didn't help, and since we hadn't met, I was not able to back Francy up with details. Tamara's response did nothing to make today less stressful."

"I could have come over to help," I say meekly, knowing that no one wants to drag a stranger into a family argument. Even if it will prove their point. Perhaps especially then. I picture how my own family would have dealt with a similar circumstance; not a pretty scenario.

"It's okay dear, it unfortunately would not have helped. She was not in a spot to listen. Which has become more common than not. It's tough on her that we chose to move. She lashes out whenever and however she can. Often at the expense of our peace," Moshe continues.

"All she does anymore," Francine murmurs in agreement. Moshe reaches over to hold her hand, gently patting her. They both fall into silence for a few breaths.

"The police want me to come by the station. There needs to be a report filed. Having you there might help. Are you free tomorrow morning?" Francine asks. Her tears have dried but her eyes now shine with the possibility of more to come.

I jump at the chance to join them. We make plans to meet in the morning and ride over together to simplify things. I fess up that I have written out what I could recall from the incident and offer to bring the notes with us. Both are delighted to have the extra help. We part ways with a hug and promise to see one another early tomorrow.

Walking back the few doors to home, I spot Brad lingering out on the small front lawn. Spotting my approach, he develops a sudden and intense interest in the solar lights I've strung through the palm on our lawn. Inspecting each connection with an unnecessary intensity.

"Busted," I whisper shout when I reach the end of our walk. He turns to look at me with an expression of mock appall on his face. I can't stop a smile from forming and give him a kiss.

"Just making sure you're okay," he quietly acknowledges, nodding slowly, then wraps his arm around me as we climb the steps into the house.

"Better. Better than I've been in a while," I reply. The honesty of it surprising me. I squeeze Brad tightly around the waist and give him a jiggle as we close the door behind us. He shakes his head and spins, twirling me in circle. We dance off into the kitchen, Brad humming a made-up song, me giggling, the dogs chiming in with a chorus of howls.

Chapter Five

The Run-in

As usual, I pushed it to the last minute to get ready. I am a woman of many flaws, but this is one of what I refer to as 'fatals'. I consistently convince myself that I have far more time than I actually do. Resulting in me dramatically flying through getting ready and leaving the house sweaty and semi-disheveled.

The question spinning around this morning is what are you supposed to wear to the police department? I stood in front of my closet for probably thirty minutes before pulling out potential choices. I don't want to be too dressed up but need to look like I care. I opt for a fitted T-shirt, loose cardigan, skinny jeans, and sandals with sparkly palm trees. Plus, these are my favorite jeans. At 5'10" it is hard to find good jeans. And by hard, I mean nearly impossible. Since it is such a challenge, wearing them always gives me a boost.

Next, I face a hair and makeup debacle. My long curly hair has, yet again, chosen to betray me. Instead of falling nicely, the curls have decided to frizz and stick out in a giant halo. It tells me we have rain on the way. My hair knows before the weather teams. The only choice is a bun. Which is approximately the size of a grapefruit and wobbles with any sudden movements. However unlikely, I hope it stays in place.

Bright and early the Cohens arrive to pick me up. Exactly on time. A skill in others that I admire.

I slide into the back seat of their pristine sedan. Francine turns, handing me a shiny cinnamon bun and hot cup of coffee when I've settled in. Not a bad welcome at all. On the way to the police department, we talk through what she is able to recall from yesterday. A solid night's rest has helped her collect her thoughts and lessened her distress. She is much sharper this morning and readily admits it. Moshe makes eye contact with me in the mirror and subtly nods.

"I know I told you a couple of times yesterday that I repeat myself," Francine says sheepishly. A slight blush on her high cheeks. "I was so embarrassed when I replayed those conversations this morning."

"You have nothing to worry about! I've told my husband the same story twice in a row," I confess and then for emphasis add, "on more than one occasion." I would like to pretend that was a white lie to make her feel better. It isn't. I'll be talking and mid-sentence remember telling Brad the same story fifteen minutes before. As intended, this makes her relax and eases some of her embarrassment.

We arrive prepared as prepared as we can be. I have my drawings and notes on the encounter neatly compiled in a small notebook. After checking in, the desk officer walks the three of us to a conference room. He doesn't seem thrilled that the Cohens have brought a non-family member along. His tone indicates we've violated some rule. An unwritten rule perhaps?

The large dingy room appears to be infrequently used by the public and is frankly a little sad. Threadbare carpet in a blue marble pattern, it is unclear if it has faded or was originally that style. The walls are painted a sickly government beige. The one only seen in social security and tax offices. There must be a massive discount on huge buckets of it, I've never seen it anywhere outside of an office like this. In the center of the room is a large table, with a chipping faux walnut veneer. The kind that catches your shirt and snags when you lean against the edge. I take a mental note to stay back from the edge when I sit. Despite the sad state of the chairs, they are surprisingly comfortable. The scratched but sturdy wooden backs, curved arm rests, and cushioned pads make leaning back away from the gross table easier than I'd thought it would be.

That is until I lean back too far and nearly topple onto the carpet.

My ear-piercing shriek brings a young female officer running through the doorway of the conference room. Instead of finding a crime in progress, she sees me clinging to the arms of the chair-gasping for breath, with a sweaty, pale face. Francine is patting my back and attempting to soothe me. Moshe is bent at the waist, leaning from his chair, and trying to pick up the contents of my bag. In my panic, I threw it up into the air, leaving the contents strewn on the floor. Not exactly the impression I wanted to give the police during our first official meeting.

Quickly assessing for threats, the officer relaxes her grip from her holstered weapon. Her tight frown is replaced by a barely concealed laugh. Displaying remarkable poise, she asks if I am okay or if she can be of assistance.

Sputtering, I do my best to explain that the chair tipped when I leaned back. I don't want to be offensive and mention my concern about snagging my shirt on the decrepit table.

"The table, right?" she asks with a smirk. "That thing is so gross. Ruined one of my best blouses leaning on it during my interview." Her Cajun drawl lengthening the sentence.

Recognizing a kindred spirit, I bark out, "OMG, it's nasty. Could they not get a better one?"

She cackles in response then fills us in with some details. We soon learn, this has been a hot topic amongst the team lately. To the point that a request for a new table has been brought to the chief with a signed petition listing over twenty names. Since we are now clearly, friends. I do a round of intros.

"I'm Cici Larkin, these are my friends and neighbors, Moshe and Francine Cohen."

"Nice to meet y'all, I'm Officer Chandra Boudreaux. New to the force and the area. I moved here about three months ago."

"I remember reading about you in the paper! Let me think," I say snapping my fingers to kick-start my brain, "you came from...Louisiana?"

"Great memory! I did. I grew up in the Bayou and was ready for a change. Needed a bit more sunshine and a bit less swamp."

"We're so glad to have you! If it doesn't creep you out, I'll give you my number, so you'll have someone local if you need it." I scrawl my number on a sticky note on the table and pass it to her. She graciously accepts it and tucks it into her pocket with a "thanks!"

Moshe and Francine are chatting with Chandra commiserating on their shared recent relocation to the area and the challenges it can bring when a sharp knock cracks at the open door. Our heads snap in the direction of the doorway. Officer Boudreaux's posture stiffens; she nods swiftly, offering a curt, 'ma'am,' then briskly departs the room without another word. She takes a post outside the open doorway, leaving it cracked open an inch or so.

A small, dark-haired woman in her thirties strides into the room. Her face is set in the sternest expression I've seen since Mrs. Archmore's in seventh grade. She takes a seat at the head of the table and lays a file folder, legal pad, and pen out in a nearly perfect line. Tapping them into place. After her precision arrangement, she makes eye contact with Francine.

In an overly loud, clear voice, she says, "I'm Detective Yoori Cho, I understand you've misplaced your wallet and would like to make a police report." She's talking so loudly and slowly that it gives the impression she thinks Francine may be deaf or perhaps unable to understand her.

The way she says "misplaced" immediately puts my hackles up.

"No, Detective Cho. I believe my wallet was stolen. That is why I have come to file a report. Not because I have misplaced my wallet," Francine responds in a calm but firm voice. Moshe reaches over and closes his hand protectively around Francine's in a gesture of solidarity. My heart warms. She has all the support she needs right there.

Detective Cho clears her throat and opens the folder in front of her. She pauses for a few seconds to sort and review the papers within. Flipping pages with a force that acts as punctuation.

In a methodical and semi-robotic tone, Detective Cho recites details, "According to the telephone report, you were unable to locate your wallet upon your return home from the bank and grocery store. When Officer Evans requested additional details, the report notes that you admit to episodes of confusion and are prone to misplace items. There was a neighbor with you at the store, you were unable to recall her name or provide contact information when asked to do so. The report notes that you became tearful, requiring the officer to speak with your husband as you were unable to continue. Am I correct? Or has the officer incorrectly recorded details of the call?" the final two questions cut like a knife. Snapping the folder closed, she returns it to its spot on the table and stares pointedly at the Cohens.

Francine is stunned. Her eyes begin filling with tears, she grips Moshe's hand tightly. He is the picture of barely contained anger-face reddened and a bulging neck vein, which appears to throb. Now is the time for me to speak.

"Detective Cho, while you may be reading directly from the report. It does not give you an accurate account of the events, only what was relayed over the phone during a time of stress. I was present and that is not exactly what happened."

"Well then, why don't you grace us with your retelling?" the snark drips from her voice. She clasps her hands in front of her on the table and she shifts from staring at Francine to making eye contact with me. Her gaze is so intense that I can feel the beads of sweat forming on my upper lip and temples.

Is this woman for real? I know my face is showing that exact sentiment. Officer Boudreaux peeks in from outside and her face mirrors mine. I swear I caught her mouthing, "what the...." as she turned away, shaking her head in confusion.

"Yet again, you are not quite correct," my gaze becomes icy and matches Detective Cho's. Refusing to blink and break eye contact, I continue, "Had you taken the time to speak with the Cohens in a decent and respectful manner, perhaps then you would have more of the facts. But since basic human decency does not seem to be in your wheelhouse. Let me straighten a few things out for you." Detective Cho leans forward to interrupt, I put my hand up to silence her.

"You may be used to bullying people into listening but today is not the day for that. You'll let me finish, then you can reassess the information relayed to you on *paper*. Please allow me to continue."

She stares at me angrily and gives an 'after you' gesture with one of her hands. "Great! Thanks for the permission. For starters, Mrs. Cohen, is not as confused as you believe, solely based on what you've read from that report. She became frustrated last night and had trouble recalling the details. That is not the same. Secondly, I was with her as she was unloading her groceries. A young man repeatedly came near to our carts and bumped into them at one point. Which was completely bizarre, there were no vehicles parked next to her. After he left, we wrapped up the conversation and parted ways. On returning home, Francine noted her missing wallet. Now, feel free to ask any questions you may have. We've also brought in some information you may find helpful."

"While I appreciate it, we won't be in need of any notes you've written. You can provide Officer Boudreaux with your description, it will be added to the report. If he or the wallet turn up, we'll contact Mr. and Mrs. Cohen," she pauses to make it clear; I will not be contacted. "But again, thank you *so* much for your help." She closes the folder and stands, signaling an end to the conversation.

"I'll leave a form on the table for you to fill in before you leave. Officer Boudreaux will collect it and escort you to the exit," She leaves the room without another word.

Francine, Moshe, and I stare at one another. Our mouths are agape, and we share similarly stunned expressions. We've clearly been dismissed. I feel a mix of anger, shame, embarrassment, and betrayal. Mostly anger, I cannot believe this woman. All total, the Detective (I hesitate to call her that), spent maybe five minutes with us. Five, very rude, minutes. Briefly I wonder if the police give out satisfaction surveys. I would love to fill one out for her. A soft knock precedes the entry of an uncomfortable-looking Officer Boudreaux. She takes a seat at the table with us.

"I am so sorry about that. There isn't a bedside manner in police work but whatever the equivalent is, she doesn't have a good one. She is nice once you get to know her though. At least, that's what I've been told," second-hand embarrassment for the behavior of her colleague written on her face. "Fill in as many details as you can on this form. It will help us with the search for the guy from the parking lot. I promise I'll do whatever I can. I plan to let my Sergeant know what went on this morning."

Leaving the form, extra paper, and pen on the table, Officer Boudreaux excuses herself to give us time to complete without interruption. We compile details based on my notes, and what Francine and I remember. The thing with his shoes though. It stays just out of memory. While I am trying to remember, I feel a hand press over mine. I glance down to see Francine's small hand resting on top of my long fingers.

She smiles and says, "I thought you may drum them right through the table. It doesn't look like it could take much more." Moshe laughs quietly to the side.

"Nervous habit," I offer as an excuse, "Tapping out a song helps me jog my memory." For emphasis, I drum my fingers on my forehead.

"Maybe I should give it a try?" Francine suggests. With a mischievous grin, she quietly taps her fingers as we return to work on the form. Moshe's deep chuckle is drowned out by my surprised laugh. Her memory may be slipping but her sense of humor seems just fine.

Within twenty minutes, we completed the form and have turned it over to Officer Boudreaux. Using the extra paper, we included a hand-drawn map of the parking lot and locations of our vehicles. Without telling Francine, I called the store yesterday to double check if her wallet had been found, also confirming the cashiers on duty, and which security company they contract with. I figure it never hurts to know a little extra. But, I opt to avoid listing any of this on the form, I don't think it will help us at this point. For now, we'll keep the list in our back pocket.

Officer Boudreaux again apologizes for Detective Cho's treatment of us and promises to speak with her Sergeant about the missing wallet. We thank her for all her help and make our way to the exit.

Slipping into the back seat of the car, my phone dings. The text reads- *Chandra* with a smiley sunshine emoji.

Maybe today wasn't a total wash after all? Could be we have a friendly police officer on our side and perhaps, a friend in the making for me?

The ride home is far less joyful than this morning. Somber is a fairly good description of the collective mood. All of us feel like we've been knocked down a few pegs. Moshe drives, staring straight out the windshield, white knuckles at ten and two on the steering wheel. Francine glumly looks out the passenger window, head tipped back in her seat, blank expression on her face. AM radio plays a talk radio show of unknown origin or content, they're babbling in the background. I text Brad paragraphs on the whole situation and how upset it's made me. Desperately trying not to cry until we're home but I can feel the tears building. The short drive seems to take forever.

Detective Cho is obviously confident that the missing wallet is no more than the actions of a confused old woman. It seems nothing we said or evidence we provided to the contrary will change her mind. I can handle people not taking me seriously, that's been the story of my life. But when I see it happening to someone else, it hurts me. I get so upset for them. I know I've got to do something. Exactly what might take me a little longer to figure out.

Pulling into my drive, Moshe puts the car into park and we sit in silence briefly. As I reach for the handle, Moshe speaks.

"Thank you for trying. It means a lot to us that you were willing to take the time and speak up for Francine. So many are willing to sweep aging neighbors under the rug or be dismissive, but you don't do that."

"I never will either. Everyone needs a voice. Especially for those of us that get ignored. Trust me, I've spent plenty of my life not being brushed aside, I'm not letting this go. Even if the police don't think this is a big issue, I do. We'll figure it out together."

Francine turns and smiles at me; she is beaming with gratitude. "Thank you for helping us."

I lean forward and pat her shoulder before exiting the car. While they back out of the drive, I stand waving goodbye.

I'm startled by an arm sliding around my waist, it only lasts for a split second. I know it's Brad without having to look.

"Thought you might need me," he quietly says while still smiling and waving. I do, I absolutely do. My fingers intertwine with his hand on my side. Once the Cohens have pulled down the block into their own drive, we turn into the house. I walk with my head on Brad's shoulder.

"Tell me how it went," he begins as he closes the door behind us. My tears are falling before the door is shut.

Chapter Six

Let the Sleuthing Begin

T alking through the events of yesterday with Brad and a good night's rest helps reset my brain. I woke up feeling refreshed and ready to tackle the day. We got up together, had our coffee on the porch, and watched the dogs play for a bit before Brad had to leave for work. With my promise I'll text any updates on the day, he reluctantly pulls out of the drive for his commute to Miami. Honking and blowing me a kiss, he's on his way.

Coco and Aggie predictably are still overflowing with energy. It is an easy decision to hit the streets for a quick walk. I pour a travel mug filled to the brim with cold brew. Hot coffee is a disaster on dog walks. Several lessons have been learned the hard way, and off we set.

I'm pulled through the neighborhood on our usual path, Aggie leading the way and Coco a nose behind. First stop is Linda's. She isn't out this early, but this minor detail doesn't stop the pups from giving her porch a once over. Just in case there is a hidden treat left out for them. Finding no treats, they cheerfully lap up water from the ever-present water dish. As they gulp the dish dry, I glance around the neighborhood. A few neighbors are out and about. Desmond is watering his lawn and waves a greeting. I return the hello and indicate we'll visit shortly.

Edna and her cronies stomp around the corner a block ahead, no doubt on the hunt for minor offenses they can use to embarrass an unsuspecting neighbor. My God, they even walk mean. How've I not noticed that before? I'll plan my walk to avoid them. To be fair, when the four of them aren't together, all but Edna are fairly decent.

Fredrick and Dina Avalon are life-long residents of the area and were welcoming when we first moved in. Hubert Walters moved here a little under two years ago, he'd been widowed a year before moving and was still in the depths of grief. He was quiet, withdrawn, but pleasant. For some reason, when combined with Edna Sparks, the claws come out and the four of them turn into the community complaint committee. Self-appointed of course.

Desmond and I spend a few minutes chatting. Mostly catching up on neighborhood news- who's out of town, in the hospital, or has company. Gerald is out of town on his grand southwestern adventure with a former college roommate. I remember now how excited he's been to see new areas of the U.S. We plan a BBQ when he's back later this week.

From there, I walk over to Francine and Moshe's house. She is sitting on her favorite glider, a mug of tea in her hand. I call out a hello as the dogs and I approach. She startles slightly.

"Good morning!" I chirp out, good mood on full blast. "Hope we didn't disturb you."

"Oh, no. You didn't dear," Francine says cautiously. She seems uncertain if she should continue. Her eyes are wide, almost owl-like.

"I've been thinking so much about yesterday and working on a plan. Detective Cho isn't likely to be helpful."

"Detective Cho...yes. He wasn't, you're right," she says haltingly and then readjusts herself on the bench breaking eye contact. Her use of 'he' gives me a pause. Does she not recall our meeting with Detective Cho?

"Good morning, Cici," Moshe calls out from the side door. "We're moving a little slow around here today." He raises his eyebrows and inclines his head to Francine and shakes his head back and forth. I take this to mean this is not one of Francine's good days with her memory. I nod back slowly in understanding. Moshe flashes me a discreet thumbs up.

"That's how most mornings are for me! We'll keep on walking and give y'all time to wake up. Enjoy the nice weather today!" I gather the dogs, and we turn to head home. Moshe mouths "thank you," as I walk past. I'll catch up with them later, there is nothing so urgent that I need to upset Francine right now.

Grey clouds have moved in, and the air gets the heavy feeling that tells you a storm is not far off. A rainy day will be perfect for putting my thoughts in order. If it is sunny, I want to be outside. The rain will keep me in and hopefully help me focus. My pups will be less enthused about the storms but are always psyched for a day of snuggling.

We make it home without running into Edna and the gang. Breathing a massive sigh of relief, the dogs and I do a celebratory dance on our way to get treats from the kitchen. Arming myself with coffee, my laptop, and a legal pad, I make a nest on the couch to get to work. Aggie and Coco are more than eager to curl up in the blanket around my legs.

Having a career in marketing has given me decent computer skills, I throw my notes and drawings into a digital format. Seeing the folder take shape gives me an odd sense of delight. I add other subfolders-locations, interviews, suspects, and miscellaneous. As if I am some sort of investigator that requires tracking all my notes. Whatever-it makes me feel better and more organized. I add in the calls and notes to the appropriate subfolders and get back to thinking about the young guy from the lot. Sipping my coffee, I try to recall as many details as possible. His shoes keep bothering me. They seemed out of place, but why? My nails drumming on the cup in a rapid-fire song and I realize it's now empty anyway. Placing it to the side, I glance at the mail on the side table. Several catalogs have piled up along with the rest of the junk and bills.

"Dress shoes!!" I shout at full volume. That is what has been bothering me. Our parking lot buddy was dressed casually except for his shoes. I can now see them clearly. A shiny, bumpy pair of dress shoes. Based on what I am remembering, they may have been alligator skin? Polished to a high shine. It was so incongruous with the T-shirt and ball cap.

Before it slips from my mind again, I add the shoes to the description. A quick internet search gives me a few options to add to the image board I've created. Trying to piece together as many things as I can before taking it back to Francine and Moshe. Having pictures to reference may help jog her memory.

Hours pass as I happily organize and research crimes in the area. I see a trend on blogs and neighborhood pages about small crimes and missing items. Am I making connections that don't exist? Potentially. At this point, making note of all of it makes the most sense to me. I can always refine it later and determine what if any could be connected. I copy links, grab screenshots, and take notes of contact information shared by posters. A few do stand out as similar to me- locations of the police reports filed and callers that were not believed due to age or medical history. Strikes a little too close to home.

My cell phone rings loudly in the kitchen. I ignore it because I am too transfixed by the task at hand. On the third round of ringing, I can no longer put off getting up to see who it is. What a day to not have my watch on! I decide to find and charge my watch. Brad is always after me to wear it anyway.

Shifting the dogs off my legs, I stand unsteadily and wait for the blood to return to my tingling feet. Really hoping this call is worth it and not calls about my non-existent car warranty. Making my way into the kitchen, the phone is ringing again. I pull it from the charger and see Francine's name on the screen. I did not expect to hear from her.

"Hey Francine!" I answer, positively delighted that she's calling. Coco and Aggie hear my excitement and join me in the kitchen, hopeful snacks will be involved. They dance and spin around my feet and I oblige each with a treat.

"Cici! I'm so glad I caught you. Moshe mentioned you'd been by this morning. I'm sorry that I missed you," Francine begins pleas- antly. Clearly, she is unable to recall my visit from earlier.

Turning to check the clock, I see it's now mid-afternoon. This must be a better time to visit. "Yes! I'm sorry we weren't able to catch up. I wanted to see if you had any more thoughts after our visit with Detective Cho. I've spent a chunk of the day putting things together."

"That's lovely dear. Unfortunately, I am not able to think of anything else. But we would love to know what you've come up with."

"Nothing concrete, just lining my pieces up. I did finally remember what was bothering me about the shoes. He was wearing these oddly shiny dress shoes."

"Yes! With pointy toes. It didn't match his outfit at all." Francine notes without a trace of sarcasm. If I'd said that, it would have come out far differently.

We discuss a few more of the notes I'd made and the similarities in other petty crimes in the area. We decide to meet tomorrow afternoon for snacks and to brainstorm at their house. She encourages me to bring the dogs. Apparently, they have a very grumpy old cat that prefers dogs over anyone else.

"It's a date!" I say and then disconnect the call. With a contented shrug, I turn back to sit on the couch. Reflecting on our call, it added such a strange twist to the day! Francine's confusion may have a pattern to it. Tracking it may prove useful. I add our conversations and the times to my notes. Time will tell if it proves to be helpful or distracting information.

As usual, I have zero plans for dinner and attempt an internet search to assist. While scrolling, I stumble upon a new restaurant that is offering a promo as a welcome to the neighborhood. Problem solved! Back to my research I go. There are a few employees from the store I wanted to talk to, as well as the bank teller. Hmmmmm...I have some more thinking to do before it's time to order dinner.

Two days later, while walking the dogs, my cell phone buzzes aggressively in the pocket of my shorts breaking the calm. Being as it is a muggy, wet morning I hold off on taking the call. It can wait until I am home. There's no sense in risking dropping my phone in a puddle. Having already ruined two that way, I've learned my lesson and am not interested in repeating those episodes. Multi-tasking is not always one of my strong suits.

The girls take their usual time sniffing around and visiting neighbors as we walk. During one of the extended sniff breaks, I use the time to take in the neighborhood. It is a quiet morning with most everyone at home. Truthfully, it is not all that uncommon in a borderline retirement community. Yes, they stay busy but in a more relaxed way than most. Mid-way down the block, there's a new car parked in front of Gerald's house. When I say new, I mean NEW. Like rolled in off the lot, shiny new. The luxury car stands out in the middle-class neighborhood. We may see the occasional Mercedes or Lexus, but a Bentley never graces these streets. I squirrel it away on my list of things to share with Brad when he gets home. He loves cars and will think it is cool that we've had one here. Part of me hopes it will still be here for him to see in person.

As we get closer, I notice Gerald's front door is opening slowly. Eager to hear how his trip went, the dogs and I pick up our pace in his direction. Before I can call out a hello, a young man exits. He is dressed in a suit and tie with dark sunglasses and carrying a small briefcase. He steps out onto the small front porch, then glances up and down the block. On seeing me, he pauses slightly before continuing down the stairs to the walkway.

Typically, I would wave a greeting but something about his demeanor makes me nervous. He makes eye contact with me while opening the car door. A shiver rolls down my spine and goosebumps tickle along my arms. Aggie and Coco utter low growls while scrabbling toward him. This man gives me the creeps! I duck my head and move along, pulling my growling dogs behind me. If it weren't raining, I would fake a photo of the dogs and snap a picture of his car. The rain will make it look too conspicuous. Mental pictures will have to do for now. My gut tells me to get away from him and go home.

Rushing in through the front door, I fish my cell from the back pocket of my soggy shorts. I half expect the call to be from either my mother or sister Cassi, we're a few days overdue for a Facetime chat. Instead, I am pleasantly surprised to see the call was from Chandra Boudreaux. No voicemail (thank God!), but a missed call and follow up text- *Do you have time for a coffee?*

First of all, when won't I make time for coffee? Secondly, I am hopeful this means she has news to share.

I shoot off a text- *always!* with a coffee cup and heart eye emoji.

After hitting send, a flood of regret washes over me. Should I be sending heart-eyed emojis to a law enforcement officer? What if this is a professional matter? We literally met a couple of days ago, while I was filling out a police report, not exactly a casual social setting. Why do I do this nonsense? Sitting and stewing, I chew my bottom lip waiting for her to respond. It's not like she's going to tell me I'm unprofessional, right?

The worrying is cut short before I can spiral too far. A meme arrives with a cat pumping both paws in the air, confetti spewing out of swirling coffee cups. Whew! Saved by a meme.

We quickly make plans to meet in thirty minutes at a Cuban coffee shop near the beach. I bound down the hall with Aggie and

Coco right behind me. While I am getting ready, I can't decide if I am more excited to find out about the case or to be grabbing coffee with someone close to my own age. Either way it's a win!

Chapter Seven

Donation to the Cause

By some miracle, the rain stopped while I was getting ready. The afternoon sun is bright and hot, absolute perfection. Chandra and I grab seats at a small table on the patio of Azúcar. The cafe has been in the neighborhood for decades and is popular with locals. Groups of elderly men gather round chess boards, while their wives talk at other tables. Young families with children, couples stopping in for a daytime date, work meetings, and the lunch crowd from nearby businesses visit the cafe from before dawn until mid-afternoon. Tables with brightly colored umbrellas attract passersby and tourists who've seen posts online. I could sit here all day and people watch. In fact, I have on multiple occasions. Another example of how I am using my unemployment to the fullest.

The waitress, a smiley early twenty-something with purple hair, and intricate floral tattoos down both arms approaches our table moments after we sit. She doesn't just appear, she actually floats up to the table.

"Welcome to Azúcar! I feel like you've been with us before?" she points double finger guns at me and smiles broadly. I nod, slightly impressed that she would recall that. It's been more than a couple of weeks since I'd been in, and that was for a to-go order. "I'm Wren, I'll be taking care of you. I hate it, but the menu is on the QR code. Take a minute and I'll be back to grab your orders." She points to the code on the table and twirls away to greet a family seated at a nearby table.

Chandra and I peruse the menu on our phones. For me, it is a complete act. As I scroll, I wonder if she can tell I'm faking. I've known what I was getting from the second we decided to come here. There are a handful of favorites that I rotate through. Today is most definitely a guava and cheese day.

Wren swings back to our table, displaying what is apparently her signature twirl. She collects our order of two Coladas, two pastries-one guava and cheese, one coconut, and promises to be back in a 'jiff.' As she turns away, I notice she's wearing roller skates. Not footwear I would expect but the twirls make more sense now.

We make small talk about the area and Chandra's relocation while waiting for our food and coffee to arrive. Once it does, we split both pastries in half and dive right in. The flaky crusts with warm sweet filling are irresistible. Each time I eat these, I feel for anyone who hasn't experienced a Cuban pastry. The strong, hot coffee balances the flavors perfectly. Absolutely magical and one of those food combos that you're not living until you've tried. Something I can never capture, nor will I attempt. I'll leave this to the experts and enjoy every morsel.

Based on the 'mmm...oh my word...mmm,' coming from Chandra, it seems safe to say she agrees with me. I can't help but smile watching her reactions. Every bite sends a tiny shower of flaky crust onto her plate. She's careful to lean forward so not a bit of it is lost. I appreciate the dedication to pastry preservation.

"It never gets old, trust me," I tell her. "No matter how many of these I've had, it's the same reaction." I lick the sticky filling from my fingers and then take a gulp of my scalding, sweet coffee to wash it down.

"We have amazing desserts in Louisiana, but I swear, I have never had anything quite like these!" She nods her head in appreciation and runs her finger along the plate to pick up the flaky bits of pastry that have fallen.

After Wren collects the empty plates, Chandra leans forward and says, "I have news..." with a conspiratorial tone.

"Please tell me you intend on sharing," I ask, my voice is a pleading singsong.

"Girl- why did you think I asked you to meet? So I could brag?" she leans back laughing heartily.

I make a "whew!" gesture and pretend to wipe my brow. She throws back her remaining coffee and pulls a water bottle with the police department logo from her purse. I stare at her with begging eyes, assuming she's taking so long for dramatic effect. Which she is. Her eyes are crinkling with pent up laughter, the rest of her face hidden by her giant water bottle.

"Okay, fine!" She relents and sits forward once more. Slowly wiping droplets of water from her lip. "I spoke with the Cohens already, right before I called you," pausing again. "We found her wallet." Her words come out as four individual sentences.

"No way! Where? Was it at the store? Or the bank?" I nearly shout; my excitement is through the roof. The caffeine from my Colada is not helping me stay calm. My body practically vibrates with my excess energy.

"That's the most interesting part. We received a call to check on a suspicious box at the Bay Side Community Center. It was left beside the donation items but something about it seemed off to the volunteers. The box was banged up and taped shut. Most donations arrive in bags or are hand delivered. The caller was concerned it was a bomb or a drug drop. When my Sargeant and I arrived, we opened the box and found it was filled with mail, papers, a couple of mostly empty wallets, house keys, and some empty watch boxes. It almost appeared to be a combined junk drawer and jewelry box."

I make an involuntary squeaking sound and clap my hands on my knees. I can barely contain myself from interrupting as she continues, "While going through the wallets, there were no ID's, cards or cash remaining. But in a couple, there were some bits of paper and receipts. We narrowed one of the wallets down to Francine by using one of the receipts, combined with the information you and the Cohens provided." At this point, I clap my hands. So happy to have had some results, even if it is the return of her empty wallet. This feels like vindication! Her wallet was obviously stolen and not simply left behind.

"Other items in the box were connected to several reports filed by folks in local communities. We were able to reunite them with property, it seems like we might be making progress."

"This is wonderful! I am so thrilled," I am grinning ear to ear. "Were there any connections amongst the owners? And why was the box at the donation center instead of thrown away?"

"Get ready, here is where it gets a little odd. Each of the reports was filed by someone over the age of seventy-five, and most were not sure if the items were stolen or misplaced. None were of a value greater than $500."

"Why does the value matter?"

"Well, if it's less than $750, it keeps it from being a felony."

"Oh!" realization dawning on me, my eyes widen at the prospect, "Do you think these are connected?"

Chandra taps the tabletop and stares off at a dog walker in the distance while she thinks. "I don't know. It seems like there are too many similarities. Unfortunately, not enough for my boss to make the official call." She slowly turns her head and makes direct eye contact. I now know why we are meeting for coffee.

"You want me to... talk to them?" My response comes out slowly with the lilt of a question at the end. Does she mean only Mr. and Mrs. Cohen or others on the list? I'm hopeful but don't want to make any assumptions.

"Unofficially," she responds and nods. "I can't ask you to investigate anything or to even help with it. What I know is your neighbors talk to you. And that may be the best we can do for now."

It is my turn to take a moment to think before I answer. This is not the turn I'd seen this conversation taking. Me? Helping the police get information? A combined dream come true and terrifying prospect. A flurry of questions enters my mind. It feels like leaves in a windstorm.

"How would I know where to begin?" I begin haltingly and start drumming out a song on the table. A list forms in my head, but knowing myself, this needs to be put on my paper before I forget. Grabbing for my bag, I rummage noisily for something to write on. Triumphantly, I hold up a pen and envelope. This will work for the moment.

"I was hoping you could start close to home," Chandra begins hesitantly. She reaches into her tote bag and pulls out a large envelope. My drumming stops as she withdraws papers.

With a swoosh, Wren reappears and gestures at the table, "Refills?"

Chandra and I mirror shrugs that indicate, why not? After placing orders for more pastries and mineral waters, we get to work. Chandra waits until Wren has skated away, then she opens the envelope. She slides out copies of newspaper clippings, a few printed pages, and some sheets of yellow legal pad paper with writing on both sides.

"Are you allowed to show me this stuff?" I whisper loudly, reaching for some of the papers and then realizing I am questioning her integrity inadvertently. The back of my neck prickles with nerves or more likely a caffeine overload.

"Oh yeah, there's nothing to worry about. All but what I've written out is public record," she nods reassuringly while organizing the envelopes contents. "My notes are just thoughts on the cases that I want to share. Not any part of the official report." Chandra has lined the papers up into five stacks. Each begins with the newspaper reports, followed by printed sheets, and ends with the handwritten notes. Despite my enthusiasm, I wait for her to take the lead on how we will proceed. The stacks may not be big, yet this feels like a big deal and it's Chandra's to share.

"The oldest report is from your neighbor, a Mr. Desmond Canistel. He phoned in a report for a missing watch," Chandra begins and slowly pushes a stack to me. "The watch was a gift from his brother. After his wife was hospitalized, and he was packing some of her belongings for the hospital when he noticed the watch missing from their shared jewelry box." She taps on an image in the printed police report. "Due to the stress of the events, he didn't think about it again for several weeks. When it sprung back to mind, he was fuzzy on the details. Mr. Canistel couldn't recall the last time he had seen or worn the watch, only the date he noticed it was missing. The officer noted his confusion in the report." She pauses to allow me to look over the report and newspaper clipping.

Without realizing it, I've begun shaking my head. Tears sting my eyes, recalling those weeks after Karen's hospitalization and all the stress Desmond was under. No wonder he wasn't sure about the last time he saw a watch; his wife had come close to death and their lives were changed forever.

"The case was not pursued beyond the initial report and promises to follow up if the item was located."

"And no one ever did until now," I murmur while still studying the reports. Chandra makes an 'uh-huh' noise and reaches for another stack.

"Next up, Mrs. Tilly Ortiz. She lives a couple of communities down from y'all," sliding the stack to me, "After a trip to the bank and post office, Mrs. Ortiz noticed her wallet missing from her purse, as well as a keepsake from her car." Chandra pauses to run her finger down the page, "Here it is, a small heart-shaped locket that hangs from her mirror. It was a gift from her husband, he died twenty-some years ago. Yet again, she could not recall the last time she saw the item, but she does recall putting her wallet in her purse after banking. Her only stop was the gas station. She withdrew a $20 bill to pay in cash. That was the last time she saw her wallet. There were no signs of a vehicle break-in."

"Let me guess, since the details weren't clear, nothing was done?" I ask, fully anticipating her answer.

"Nailed it! Should we move onto case three?" Chandra asks and pushes the stack to me. I greedily accept the papers and begin an initial run through.

"This is Ms. Linda Langston," Chandra starts.

"Please no, not Linda! There's no way anyone could accuse her of being elderly and confused."

"Well, they did. She called to report missing jewelry, it is listed on the report. Mostly again, of sentimental value, not monetary. She was clear in her descriptions and value, but since she could not recall when they were last seen," Chandra trails off, she lifts her hands and shrugs.

"This is getting tiresome and frustrating. Let's move through the next two so I can be good and mad," I sigh loudly and slap the papers back onto the small table.

Chandra moves through the next two cases quickly. Mr. Abraham Barlowe, an eighty-eight-year-old veteran who reports his wedding ring and two medals are missing. He has no previous issues with his memory. Finishing with Mrs. Viola Katz, a seventy-nine-year-old widow with known memory loss after a battle with cancer. She reported the loss of a purse containing a wallet, cell phone, and a few bracelets. I hide my face in the reports momentarily to collect myself and get my thoughts in some semblance of order.

"Whoa gals! You've got serious business happening here," a deep male voice interrupts my brain break. Chandra and I turn our heads to see a tall, tattooed guy standing at the table. His glossy black hair shines in the sunlight, and his deep brown eyes sparkle with delight. He's holding a tray of pastries and two sweating bottles of mineral water. Chandra's jaw is nearly on the table.

"Always! This is the place to come for serious work." I tease in return, while making space on the table. His full attention turns to Chandra.

"I'm Seb, I don't think I've seen you here before," he says with a toothy smile.

"I'm...Chandra..." she squeaks out slowly. I kick her under the table to keep her talking. "This is my first time here, loving it so far and more by the minute," a blush creeps from her neck up to her high cheeks. Neither of them breaks eye contact.

"Lucky for us!" he responds and winks as he walks away.

Chandra folds her hands over her face, and she groans with embarrassment. "Could I have been more awkward?"

I laugh and poke her in the shoulder, "It wasn't as bad as you're picturing, I promise!" She continues to shake her head. "Eat some pastry, you'll feel better."

"Doubtful. That one is going to keep me awake for a few nights," she moans, reaching for the plate.

While she nibbles, I once again flip through the reports and clippings. Feeling satisfied that the details are solidly in mind, I reach for her notes. She's thorough in her personal coverage of the reports and has recorded her insights on the officers involved- times, dates, and neighborhoods. There's already been so much work done; I am not certain how much help I'll be.

"You've got everything we could ask for here. What did you have in mind for me?" I swig from my water and grab a bite of pastry. Hoping the movements will distract from my nervousness.

Still chewing, Chandra mumbles, "Talk to them," and holds up her finger for me to wait. Swallowing with a gulp, she continues, "After their stellar interactions, they aren't really interested in talking to the police right now. They've given the information as it is remembered. When I called, they were expecting an update. Every call led to disappointment. I'm hoping, since you're their neighbor, they may want to talk with you. If we can get them to open up, we may be able to help."

I nod in agreement and consider her request. Talking with a friendly face that they know personally, or a mutual connection might be just what is needed.

"Should we start with the oldest report? I am happy to talk with Desmond this evening or tomorrow."

Chandra grins and gives me a high-five across the table. "How about tomorrow? Then you'll have time to think about what you'll say."

We begin planning conversation openers while finishing our treats. It doesn't take us long until the plates are wiped clean. A gravelly, grinding sound hints of Wren's imminent arrival.

"Hey gals! Thanks for swinging by. I'll leave your checks, and you can pay when you're ready," she hands a bill to each of us. Then leans down and whispers, "Check the back" to Chandra. Then spins away with a small wave and giant smile.

"What in the world?" Chandra holds up her check to reveal Seb's name and number with a smiley face. She is clearly thrilled. We dissolve into a fit of giddy giggles. Who knew today would turn out like this?

Chapter Eight

Neighborly Chats

While I am eager to chat with Desmond and Linda, I need to ease into the day. Diving straight in won't help any of us. Using Brad's morning off, we choose to start our day with breakfast at a favorite cafe before I move into questioning our friends and neighbors. Brenda's Bakery makes the best sandwiches on fresh bagels, brioche, or croissants. Completely irresistible. Brioche toast with scrambled egg, thick cut smoked bacon, gouda, and avocado for Brad. Plain bagel, egg with a runny yolk, savory sausage, and ghost pepper cheddar cheese for me. Locally roasted coffee with cream and a little bit of Florida sugar. The perfect touch to wrap up a heavy breakfast.

We grab the sandwiches to go and drive a few blocks over to the beach access. A perk of living here is going to the beach whenever it feels right. Brad grabs a blanket from the back of the car and I gather breakfast.

Our usual spot is a broad sandy patch off the walkway. Far enough from the path and water that we can relax in peace without getting sand kicked on us or caught in the low waves. We eat in the quiet of the beach. Sea grasses dance behind us, whispering together. Gulls call out overhead. Waves are crashing on the shore. The most calming sounds on earth.

An unforeseen blessing of losing my job is this kind of morning. When I worked in the city, there was never time for breakfast together on weekdays. Brad's schedule has far more flexibility than mine ever did. I crumple up the sandwich wrapper, tucking it under my leg, and lean against Brad's shoulder. He is still finishing but taps his head on mine and wraps his left arm around me. We sigh in unison. Having a morning to relax was needed.

For the next hour or so, we watch the beachgoers and make up stories of their lives to entertain ourselves. Here is one thing I adore about my husband, his complete and utter silliness. On the outside, he is quiet, kind, and mild mannered but with me he is an absolute goober with a wicked sense of humor. Few get to glimpse of this side of him. I consider it a privilege.

After breakfast, we vote to take a walk along the water. I go over my plan for *casual* conversations with our neighbors. About stuff that is none of my business and potentially embarrassing for them. Nothing could go wrong, right?

Returning home, I leash up Coco and Aggie, taking time to coordinate their harnesses and bandanas. The girls will be a critical part of the ruse and I need them to be at maximum cuteness levels. Our neighbors (at least the ones I'm talking with) love them. Walking the dogs will be a natural conversation opener, especially if they're dressed up.

Brad gives me a parting kiss to wish me well during my chats. Originally, I'd planned to start with Desmond then go to Linda. Once I leave the house things change, the dogs make a beeline for Linda's. She's on the porch, sipping coffee and throws her hand up to wave, welcoming me to join her. No way I can pass that opening by. I chuck my plans out the window and steer the dogs her way, waving like a maniac. Thankfully, this behavior will not seem out of the ordinary in her eyes.

I study Linda as I walk toward her porch. Taking in details of her for my notes. Tall and average build, shoulder length wavy dark-gray bob, with a few bright silvery streaks. Linda still looks very much like a teacher, despite having retired several years ago. She rotates through a dozen pairs or more of brightly colored reading glasses, when not in use, the pair hang on a beaded cord around her neck. She dresses in pressed chinos and twin sets or cheery blouses. Her jewelry is minimal, leaning toward artsy but never flashy. I wonder which pieces were taken and struggle to call up the pictures from memory.

"There's my girls!" Linda calls out as we reach the end of her walk. I release their leashes, and the dogs run straight to her. Linda must be grateful for the lack of mud. Her white slacks are now patterned with tiny wet paw prints. Both dogs have jumped onto her lap and are slathering her with kisses. I don't intervene. In the past, Linda has scolded me for telling the dogs to get down. She adores them and soaks up all the love they have to offer, which is a lot.

I sit in a chair next to Linda and watch with delight as she talks with the dogs then tucks one on each side of her lap. Cooing over their outfits of the day. Coco wears a neon pink, ruffled harness and a bandana with brightly colored fruit slices. It complements her caramel coat. Aggie sports a similar outfit, in lime green. This ensemble complements her fluffy white coat. All three appear to smile when they turn to face me. I snap a picture, it's too cute to resist. They look so pleased with themselves! I send a copy to Linda. She enjoys posting these moments to Facebook for her friends and family, she says, 'it helps them see I'm not shriveling and lonely.' Which always makes me giggle. She's so saucy! I cannot imagine anyone thinking she's confused or impaired.

We chat about life updates. She shares about a recent trip she took to New Orleans with former colleagues, how her family has been, and a community fundraiser we've been enlisted to assist with.

"Ack! I've done all the talking. It feels like weeks since we've caught up and I got carried away. Tell me, what have you been up to?" she asks with a look of genuine interest on her face. I couldn't have planned a more perfect way to kick this off. I internally celebrate, pleased with an unexpected opening.

"Well, you heard about poor Francine's wallet theft?" I begin, a little nervous. My throat feels tight, and I know my voice sounds pinched.

"I did! It was so fortunate that you were with her. The poor dear," Linda shakes her head with pity. Her eyes are downcast, she's begun twirling Aggie's curls along her collar.

"It really was. The police weren't inclined to believe her. They seemed to think because she gets confused that she simply misplaced the wallet," I pause, trying to give Linda an opening to talk. She's now twirling faster and looking at the Cohens house with her brow furrowed. She seems to be on the cusp of speaking.

"Did your dogs poop on my lawn?" a shrill voice pierces the silence. We spin in unison to see Edna in the middle of Linda's sidewalk. She's holding a plastic grocery sack in the air, shaking it angrily. I'm horrified by the sight and irritated that she's intruded.

"No, Edna. My dogs did not poop on your lawn," the disdain for this woman apparent in my tone. I shake my head in disgust. "Put that bag down before you spill it."

"Don't you lie to me!!!" she shouts, shaking the bag more aggressively. Her face reddens and she stomps her foot.

"Edna- that is enough. I saw Cici and the dogs leave the house and walk straight here. I must insist you take the bag of feces and leave my lawn immediately," Linda says coolly. Her voice is so chilling, it leaves no room for argument. Edna stomps her foot again but turns and leaves without another word. Crossing the street, she throws the bag onto my front lawn then scuttles off to her house.

"That woman is a boil on this neighborhood. The tone of civility has gone downhill since she moved here," Linda disappointedly notes.

"I have to agree with you. When Brad and I moved here, this was the sweetest community. We were shocked to be surrounded by such loving neighbors. It seemed we'd found a ready-made family. Over the last few years, things really have changed. People have left, new folks have moved in. The trusting and friendly community feeling isn't there. Except for a few of us," I reach over and pat her hand. She smiles at me. But her smile seems sad, and her eyes shine with tears. I believe I may have inadvertently opened the conversation for us.

"You're so right," Linda shifts Coco and withdraws a tissue from the pocket of her sweater. She dabs at her eyes and nose. "I can sympathize with Mrs. Cohen." My breath catches, and I force myself to wait for her to continue. I don't want to give away information or take away her moment of sharing. There's something she needs to get off her chest.

"A few months ago, I noticed some items missing from my jewelry box. Nothing of major value. Mostly items left to me by family members. Costume jewels really. But every piece meant something to me," she pauses to wipe her nose. I lean forward, offering more support. She squeezes my hand tightly.

"Once I noticed all that was missing- a brooch, bracelets, earrings, and a few pins, I launched an all-out search of the house. I could not find them anywhere. My sister in Kansas and I talked, and I decided to file a police report," her voice tenses, "What a mistake that was! The officer made me feel like a foolish old woman. He asked when they'd gone missing, where I'd seen them last. I had no idea, you see they're never worn. It is jewelry that is far out of style and sentimental. Rather than acknowledge the validity of it all being rarely used, I was brushed aside like I am some demented and incapable woman. I was so hurt, that I've not talked about it much. It was humiliating," she sobs and places her free hand over her eyes.

I jump from my chair and wrap my arms around her, enveloping her and the dogs in a hug. They sense her distress and begin licking her face and hands while burrowing into her neck. Seconds later, she's laughing and puts her arms around us all.

"Why didn't I tell you sooner?" she says through the giggles and tears. "I could have felt better."

I smooch her on the top of her head and retake my seat.

"You should have! If nothing else, we could have talked about it. You didn't have to deal with it alone," my voice is thick with emotion. The strain she must have felt over the last few months weighs heavily on me. Knowing another one of my friends has been brushed aside makes me angry and pushes me to do more. This isn't ok and I can't let this go. "I'm helping the Cohens a bit with the theft of her wallet, and we were able to provide details to the police. Details that were actually helpful. Would you be okay if I took a little time and looked into your missing jewelry?" I fall short of calling it an investigation, which seems too presumptuous.

Linda doesn't seem surprised at all. She slowly nods her head while thinking. When she turns to face me, her sad smile has been replaced with a hopeful one, "I wouldn't mind at all."

I breathe a sigh of relief. This could have gone several ways, and this is honestly the best outcome. Should I bring up that the police have unofficially asked me to investigate the thefts? That I knew about it already? Before I can speak, Linda does.

"You should probably talk to Desmond too."

"Desmond?"

"Yes. After I contacted the police, I was devastated and embarrassed. The next afternoon, I visited Karen and Desmond to check in and see if they needed anything. He noticed something was off. The following day, he invited me over for tea. The story came pouring out. He shared he'd had a similar encounter after reporting the theft of a watch," Linda tells me. She is picking at the tissue in her hand, pulling tiny pieces of it free and piling them up. She seems nervous to be sharing this.

"I won't let him know it came from you," I offer.

"No, it should be fine. Can I call him first?"

"Of course! However you'd like to handle it," I quickly respond, still surprised by how today is going. Pushing it, I take it one step farther. "Have you heard of this happening to anyone else?"

"I don't know any personally, but I've heard rumors of others nearby. Desmond might know more when you talk to him," she suggests. "Maybe, when I call, I can ask him for you?"

"You're the best Linda! I want to help however I can. This all feels so unfair, and I want to help sort it out."

"Hang on, I'm going to call Des," she excuses herself and goes into the house.

The dogs trot after her inside, like they live here. They've got some nerve, but their audacity pays off as the door clicks closed behind them. I'm left to sit alone on the porch. Using my time wisely, I make notes on my phone and send an update to Brad.

Me- *Hey Babe! She's in :) Too much to text.*

Brad- *So proud of you! I knew it'd go well. Can't wait to hear deets. Be safe.*

Me- *Te amo*

Brad- *Te amo muito*

I title the note, *Linda,* and start laying a framework from the basics of our conversation. More details can be added when I am home. Lost in thought, I feel something cold press into my ankle. I shriek and nearly throw my phone. Aggie has rejoined me on the porch. She must have pushed the door back open and nose bumped me for attention.

A startled Linda appears at the door with a cordless phone held to her face. I mouth, "I'm okay," and gesture to Aggie. She gives a thumbs up and turns back inside. The call seems to be taking longer than I'd thought it would. Perhaps Desmond isn't as interested in sharing? Pondering that possibility, I continue jotting my thoughts down from our chat until Linda rejoins me.

Sighing loudly, she flops into her chair. She takes a deep breath and slowly pushes it out through pursed lips. Experience has shown that when someone needs to implement deep breathing techniques, things are not going well. Two more rounds of deep breaths and Linda is ready to speak.

"Well..." she starts slowly, "that didn't go quite like I thought it would."

"Uh-oh..." is all I get out before she holds her hand up to quiet me.

"Desmond is fine speaking with you. He is actually pleased to do so. The police have located his watch but have remained otherwise unhelpful. There is a larger issue at hand," she again pauses for a couple of slow breaths. Her neck and face are mottled with emotion. I find myself holding my breath, waiting for her to continue. She inhales sharply and says, "Desmond has been in contact with fourteen other victims of similar crimes within the county."

"FOURTEEEN!" I exclaim.

"Yes, fourteen," a quiet voice says from the porch stairs, Desmond has joined us. "Please do your best to keep your voice down," he cautions me, "This is sensitive for many of us. There have been more than the sixteen instances, but some have chosen not to file reports after speaking with friends."

I stare in shocked silence. How can so many have had thefts or break-ins, and the police are chalking it up to confusion in the elderly? These folks have been let down. Whether Chandra wants my help or not, I'm giving it.

"Let's go inside to speak privately," Linda suggests. As we stand to walk inside, I notice Gerald's creepy visitor once again at his home. Who is this person? Why is he there all the time? He sees me looking his direction, rather than wave or smile in greeting, he simply stares at me. I cannot see his eyes behind the sunglasses, but it gives me chills nonetheless. I quickly turn to follow Linda and Desmond in the house, noticing they each have a dog tucked in their arms. I push the door closed and turn the lock quickly, there's a sense of urgency to put space between us and the visitor.

We sit in Linda's kitchen; she brews tea and puts out a plate of scones for us to snack on. When everyone is settled, I ask Desmond if he can share more of what is going on. I open my note app and prepare to type.

"You might want to record this instead," he gestures to my phone resting on the table. Wordlessly, I open a voice note and hit record.

Chapter Nine

Connecting the Dots

A week later and I've got a lunch date. Pulling my Jeep into the *Pelican's Beak,* I park toward the back of the lot. For once in my life, I was out of the house early, packed everything I needed, and am dressed in a presentable fashion. Usually, one or more of these are missing. I can be on time but not have what I need AND look presentable. You have to make choices. Today is different though. Desmond has arranged for me to meet four of the theft victims. Time to act like I have it together.

Arriving early gives me the opportunity to preview who I'll be meeting with. About ten minutes before our lunch reservation, they begin trickling in. Instead of entering the restaurant, they meet as a group and talk briefly in the lot. All of them exchange hugs. My heart again hurts for their troubles.

I snap a couple of photos with my phone, mostly for my own notes but consider that these also may be interesting to Chandra or the hateful Detective Cho. Once all have gone into the restaurant, I move my car from the back end of the lot, toward the front and make my way inside. Hoping this little deception will make it seem that I've just arrived.

Desmond waves me to a large table in the back corner of the brightly lit diner. All seats are occupied but mine. Introductions are made and soon the group is chatting happily. Almost as if they've forgotten why we're together. Around the table is not a group of confused, elderly people who misplace items at random. Rather, I find a sparkling group of long-time friends, engaging in rapid fire conversation. Interrupting them seems impossible, mostly because I'm invested in the stories they're telling.

Tilly is the first to share her story. She has lived in the area for sixty years. Her family relocated from Texas for her husband's job when her oldest girls (identical twins) were in junior high. Instantly the entire family fell in love with Florida and felt at home in their new city. Her four daughters all live nearby with their families. Her family has grown, in total, she has eleven grandchildren, and four great-grandchildren. Despite their numerous offers, she has chosen to continue living alone. She teases that her baby is now on the cusp of retirement and threatening to move into her neighborhood. Tilly enjoys the peace and quiet that comes from being solo. While running errands a few months ago, she noticed something was off.

"I'd run a full day of errands, or what feels like a full day at ninety-three," she begins with a chuckle, and the others around the table share the laugh with her. "A trip to the post office, followed by the bank, and then to fuel up my old beast. Mind you, $20 doesn't go as far as it used to, but I am a creature of habit. I put in $20 in cash, the same as I do every time. When I got home and was settling in for the evening, I went to pay some bills and noticed my wallet was missing. I searched all through the car and couldn't find it. One of my granddaughters, Elena, happened to stop by to visit, she helped me look and noticed my little heart charm missing from my mirror. It wasn't worth much but was a gift from my Danny. He's been gone for sixteen years. Having it with me in the car brings me comfort." Tilly holds up a picture on her phone. "This is Danny and I on our wedding day. He gave me a bracelet as my 'something new' that morning. The charm hung from that bracelet." She turns her phone back and smiles wistfully at the image. Her thumb rubs to touch the image of his face before she rests her phone back on the table.

"We looked all over the car and house. Elena finally called her mother, and we decided to call the police. The officer that took the call was very friendly with her but when he spoke with me, it all changed. He was unkind and treated me like I was daft. He kept saying, 'Are you *sure* you didn't just lose it?'" her voice changes to mimic a whiny, mocking tone. "It was so offensive. Elena was extremely upset when I told her what happened. She wished I'd let her speak to him, but it was over and done with by then. The officer promised he'd call if they located any of my items. I heard nothing until the call earlier this week." She shakes her head, a mixed expression of sadness and frustration spread across her face.

"Thankfully, I have the support of a family that was ready to fight for me. Many are not that fortunate," heads around the table nod in agreement.

Emboldened by Tilly, a frail woman speaks up from the other end of the table. She's so petite that she could be described as bird-like. At our introduction earlier, I was nervous to shake her hand for fear of harming her. But Alma Brittman's looks are deceptive. Her tight, sharp grip was similar to a vice wrapped around my hand. I lean in as she begins speaking, I don't want to miss a word.

"I wish my story had a different ending, but it doesn't," her voice is small and thin, but laced with the slow drawl of her native Georgia. "My late husband's watch, a pin from the early days of my nursing career, and an extra set of checks went missing. I noticed after returning home from a cruise with my sister and cousin. The cad of an officer I reported it to questioned my sanity a half dozen or more times! I was madder 'an a wet hen when I got off the phone," her irritation still clear in the retelling.

"You're telling me! The officer I spoke with was unbelievably rude. The little twerp," a gruff voice, thick with years of smoking, chimes in. Marvin Holzer, a retired firefighter from New Jersey, shares his story next. He's a large, physically imposing man with a laugh that rumbles like thunder. "I called to report loss of a Saint Michael medallion. It was passed down for two generations. After retiring, I keep it on the post of my bed, reminds me of all the scrapes I got out of, ya know?"

He looks past us all, as if recalling events he's lived through. Then in an instant, he snaps back to finish his story. "I noticed it missing when I was changing the bed sheets. I could have sworn it was there the night before but wasn't certain. It is one of those things, you get so used to seeing it that you no longer notice it. Panic set in when I realized it was gone. I called the cops right away and they treated me like a putz. Man, I tell you, was I livid. Filled that cop's ears with what I thought of him. Did no good though," he smacks a palm on the table, rattling the dishes. The shame and frustration of the memories vivid in his mind.

"Mine doesn't have any spectacularly different details," Eleanor Speer, a mild-mannered and even tempered, ninety-six-year-old, with a classic old Florida drawl says quietly. "I began to notice a few missing items, bracelets, earrings, a gold pen, and finally a credit card. The officer was not overly enthusiastic about the thefts. Instead, he implied that I had simply forgotten where I'd placed them. Honestly, it hurt to have my age used against me. 'Ms. Speers, could you simply have forgotten?'" she intones in a simpering voice.

"He doesn't know me but choses to believe I must have dementia since I am well past ninety." As she says these final words, the others nod in solidarity. Marvin raises his Diet Coke with a booming, "Here, here!"

Desmond shares that since their last meeting, another victim of thefts, Franklin Mercer, has died. I gasp in horror, picturing another crime having befallen him. Linda jumps in quickly to explain, "No need to panic dear. He was admitted to the VA Hospital after a stroke and died in the hospital. His nephew made it in time from Arkansas to spend time with him before he passed. We're grateful he wasn't alone." Murmurs of agreement again sound around the table.

"Viola Katz has been admitted to a memory care center here in town. Her family felt she was no longer safe to be at home after a small fire. She wasn't injured thankfully, but it was the final straw. Over the last few years, her memory has worsened and she's really safest at the center," Linda says, sadness heavy in her voice.

"I've known Viola for thirty years; the cancer really took it out of her. She wasn't the same after," Tilly adds and dabs at the corner of her eye with her napkin. Linda reaches over to squeeze Tilly's hand. The two share a moment of silent reflection for their friend.

"Thank you all for sharing with me. I am so sorry to hear how you were treated when you asked for help," my voice cracks with emotion. Seeing their faces and hearing their stories has taken more of a toll than I thought it would. "With your permission, I'd like to spend time looking into each of the events and see if I can find any helpful information. The police will, of course, continue the official investigation. I want to help fill in the gaps. For you, your family, or the police. Would that be alright with you?"

"You've got my vote!" Marvin half-shouts and claps me on the back. The remaining guests around the table all begin speaking at once, in agreement.

I can't help grinning and thanking them profusely. That they are willing to trust me with this is mind boggling. I start collecting contact information from all but Desmond and Linda and figure out the best times to meet based on vacations, cruises, and social commitments. This is one busy group of people! In the back of my mind, I am freaking out a little. Chandra is going to lose it when I tell her about today. We've got a way bigger problem than we thought. We're going to need re-enforcements for sure.

"Cheer up darlin, you'll get to the bottom of it. We have faith in you," Alma encourages me, she offers a wide smile. She must see a glimpse of my internal conversation on my face. I do my best to calm those inside voices and plaster a relaxed (more likely maniacal) smile on my face.

After the plates have been cleared and checks paid, we make promises to be in touch soon and part ways. Once in my car, I shoot off texts to Brad and Chandra. Both have been texting me all through lunch for updates. Brad will be stuck in meetings until the end of his day, but Chandra is off this afternoon.

As I leave the lot, I decide to call Chandra. She's been desperate to hear how it's gone. Before the first ring has finished, she answers with, "What did they say? I need to know it all!"

I cackle instead of responding which only aggravates her, "Cici! I swear, if you don't tell me something my head is going to pop clean off!"

"Okay, fine," I relent, "Do you want coffee at my house, or do you want try to bump into Seb again?"

"He can wait, text me your address and I'll meet you there."

She must be desperate if she doesn't want to attempt a chance encounter with Seb. At the first red light, I send her my address and share my location. For someone who can never remember to tell people when they'll be arriving or if they're home safe, location sharing has become my life saver.

Chandra responds- *Got it, see you in 12 minutes.*

My lord, the precision. No time for messing around on the way home. She apparently means business. I can see how this friendship will go- me eternally late and Chandra waiting for me.

I take the fastest way home and hit most of the lights green. Turning into my subdivision, I am celebrating my success. Which quickly turns to defeat, Chandra is already in front of the house. She's leaning on her car. A purple 4-door Jeep with no top or doors. Not exactly the car I'd imagined for her.

"Interesting..." I mutter, walking past her to the front porch.

"Shut it. I'm living my Beach Barbie dreams," she sticks her tongue out and hip checks me as she passes me on the stairs.

"Noted, Miss South Beach," I tease while unlocking the door. Coco and Aggie rush to the door barking furiously. I can't even get their names out before Chandra has dropped to the floor and scooped one up under each arm. They wriggle with delight and kiss all over her face. She giggles and returns their kisses.

"I LOVE them!" she exclaims between puppy kisses. "I've missed my Grandmama's tiny dogs. This is what walking in the house should feel like." The trio dances in a circle while she kicks off her sandals. I can't decide who is happier that she's here. Despite the dogs over-the-top exuberance, I think it may actually be Chandra.

"You've got new best friends, and they may never let you leave. Have a seat while I start some coffee," I gesture out through the sliding doors to the lanai.

"Don't have to tell me twice!" Chandra makes a beeline for the door, toting both dogs. They've calmed slightly since we first entered and are now resting like furry footballs with wagging tails and happy squeaks.

I join Chandra and the dogs with two mugs of steaming coffee and a plate of macarons. When I set them on the table between us, she does a little dance in her chair.

"Did you make these?" she asks, gesturing at the delicate and colorful cookies. Without waiting for my answer, she places a chocolate macaron on her napkin.

"Oh dear lord, no!!" I exclaim, "I can bake one thing- key lime pie. That's literally it," I confess with a shrug. "These are a thank-you gift from Linda Langston." With a huge smile, I grab one of the earl grey and lavender macarons. Taking a small bite, I savor the sweetness with the bit of tang from the bergamot.

"I was about to be seriously impressed! Macarons are not for the faint of heart and take skills. Thought maybe you were holding out on me," she sneaks a second cookie from the plate while talking. A soft lemony yellow with white filling in the center. "Gah!! That's amazing, it's lemon and vanilla." Obviously, Linda has another super fan in the making. Her baking skills rival many professionals in the area.

"Can you believe she makes these for fun? Simply for the joy of baking," I say shaking my head, all while nibbling a mint and chocolate version. "A concept that is completely foreign to me."

"Let her know, I am always happy to taste test whenever she needs," Chandra says cheerfully, fingers swirling over the remaining cookies, while she plans her selection.

"I will! She was so appreciative that we're taking time to help. She'll probably flood you with treats."

"Way to bring that back around, I am dying to hear how lunch went. The cookies totally knocked me off track. But I'll do my best to focus," she slides two more onto her plate.

"Believe it or not, that was not intentional," I say with a laugh. "Pretty sure there's way more to this than we realized in the beginning."

I pull up my notes app and get busy. While relaying each of their stories, Chandra takes notes on her own phone. The timelines are especially interesting to her. Not everyone was able to recall exactly when they made the initial reports, but the general dates are helpful enough.

"If there are nineteen known events, who's to say there aren't more?" I wonder aloud. Tapping my nails while I think.

"You may be onto something," Chandra adds. "There seems to be a trend with the reports being taken on the afternoon shift. The officer seems to treat everyone similarly. Questioning their competence."

"It feels like it's planned, right?" I probe.

"There's a definite scripted feel to it. Almost like how to handle the calls has been decided. Take the report, question their memory of events, downplay the legitimacy, and make empty promises to follow up."

"Is it me or did you just write out their formula? Everyone shared nearly that exact structure with me," the concern over this being done intentionally mounting.

"Did you happen to catch the officer's name?"

"No, but every instance involved a male officer. And oddly, everyone mimicked a whiny, nasal voice. So, either they copied each other's tone...."

"Or he really sounds like that..."Chandra finishes my sentence and her voice fades. She chews the cap of her pen. The crunching blends with my drumming fingers. It makes me giggle.

"What? What's funny?" Chandra asks.

"Nothing. We're just noisy thinkers," I smile, wiggling my fingers at her.

"You're a nerd, anyone ever tell you that?"

"All the time, it's what makes me delightful."

"Noisy thinking aside, we've learned there are way more incidents than we knew of. Reports consistently are in the evening, male officer, potentially with a nasal voice. Dude is either part of something or has major beef with the elderly," Chandra sums up the information tidily. "Only one was taken by Levan Evans. He doesn't match that voice though."

"What will you do with this?"

"For starters, I'm taking it back to Sergeant Lawrence. He's my mentor and boss. He'll know what we should do about it. After that, I assume we'll take it to Detective Cho together."

"Ugh! Her name makes my blood boil. Do you even think she'll care? She was so awful to the Cohens," I recall bitterly. Still pondering all the things I wish I'd have said to her when we met last.

"She's actually not all that bad after all. Since you had your run-in, I've had a few meetings with her. I'm pretty sure the ice queen routine is a show," noting my disbelief, she continues, "Cho seems to be a nice person for the most part. Which I didn't see coming."

"Well, I'll believe it when I see it," I pout and fling back in my chair. Fully feeling like a bratty teen. My mind is made up and I have no intention of changing it.

"Either way, she has to know about it. Sarge will help me get the notes in order before we give them to her. Although, it might make the most sense to have him go over it. Might have a bigger impact."

"I know there's probably hierarchy stuff at play, but don't undersell yourself. You're putting in the work, you should get to tell her."

"In all fairness, you're doing a lot of it," she acknowledges with a sheepish smile.

"I'm happy to! Seriously though, you take the cred. I don't want any of the spotlight. You don't need to bring me up unless you think it's necessary," I insist.

"Making zero promises, it feels wrong not to share that you're helping. I wouldn't know even half of what I do if it weren't for you. But you're right that in the first meeting, it may not be wise to bring it up."

"You get to make that call," I reply with a smirk, eager to pass that baton off to her.

The remainder of our coffee chat is spent catching up on life and news. Yes, it's only been a few days since we hung out, but Chandra has updates. She and Seb have started *talking*. The way she re-emphasizes *talking* in a super dramatic way that hints at far more.

They've got an official date scheduled for Friday night. We go over the menu in detail, plan potential outfits, and in general revel in the thrill of a first date.

Chapter Ten

Selfie with a Bit of Spying

Chandra heads home and I am left alone to plan dinner. Groaning aloud, I yet again regret my failure to plan. This is my eternal battle- what will I make, and will I ruin it? The internet was no help, I haven't seen Mirabel in days, my sister didn't answer the phone. Phoning a friend has not been helpful. Meaning my only options are continuing to scroll or cobble together a meal from what I find in the fridge. Historically, this ends in disaster. But I am no quitter, so I'll keep trying to make it happen.

Dreading the task, I crank up a nineties pop channel and get to work, rooting through the fridge. Praying inspiration hits while I scrounge around. There has to be something in here. I adore grocery shopping, so there isn't a shortage of options. Simply of creativity.

By the time Brad arrives home, I've miraculously figured it out and am pretty proud of dinner. This may be the first time a thrown together meal has not been a flop. When the front door opens, I call out, "Out back!"

The fans are on, and the evening is pleasantly warm. A breeze ripples through the plants along the fence. Nature is helping to set a relaxed tone for dinner.

"Wow! I didn't expect this," Brad exclaims when he crosses the doorway.

I've set the table with our good dishes, a set we were gifted years ago for an anniversary. The dishes are pale turquoise with a gold rim on the ruffled edges, giving the impression of a seashell. To add light (and fight our hummingbird-sized mosquitos), there are candles and lit torch lights. On a large platter in the center, I've plated grilled chicken with lemon and herbs. Warm pita, a Greek yogurt-garlic sauce, hummus, feta, chopped fresh radishes and mint are arranged on smaller dishes. A cold bottle of white wine sits between two glasses.

"Is there an occasion I missed?" genuine confusion passing over his face. The fear all husbands face at some point in marriage.

"Nah! Creativity struck when I was riffling through the fridge. Decided to go with it and see what happened. And here we are," I wave my hand over the spread on the table. I can't keep the pride from my voice. Nothing is burnt or undercooked, the food goes well together, and no smoke detectors are alarming. A win all around!

"It smells amazing!" his stomach growls to emphasize the point.

We each take a seat and begin dishing up food. The dogs take up their posts on the chaise lounge, ever hopeful there will be leftovers for them. No matter how badly dinner turns out, one of them will always eat it. Brad immediately starts in on his plate, a pita loaded with chicken and all the toppings on the table. His eyes widen and he stops chewing mid-bite. I get nervous- what could possibly be wrong?

"Are you okay?" I almost don't want to know what's wrong with the food.

"Ha! I'm totally fine, just enjoying my dinner," he mumbles around a mouth stuffed with pita. I smile at him, thankful as always that he eats no matter what I give him. But tonight, I actually believe the compliment. My own pita is fantastic. Tucking this meal idea in my back pocket. Quick, easy, and delicious- precisely what I'm always searching for.

Dinner was a huge boost to my confidence. I'd been doubting myself all afternoon. Thinking maybe I should return to marketing and abandon working on the missing items. Making a successful (and delicious) dinner put me back on track. I can do things even if

I am uncomfortable. A simple meal might seem unequal to the task of helping our friends, but in my mind, it is a huge deal.

As we do the dishes, I tell Brad all about lunch and my follow up coffee with Chandra. He is as shocked as we were by the number of folks involved.

"I thought there were the original five, plus the dozen or so Desmond mentioned?" he asks to clarify, a macaron in one hand and coffee in the other.

"Right! Chandra came to me with the five police reports. Desmond knew of fourteen more. But I get the feeling there are even more that we don't know about yet."

"How are you going to find out?"

"Chandra is going to pull the reports and look for similarities. We have a baseline description of the officer taking the calls, based on his voice and the time of day. Once she knows more, she'll take it to her Sergeant."

"Is she mentioning you or keeping you out of it for now?"

"We agreed that it is probably best to not bring me up until it's necessary."

"I prefer that too. No need to add drama to our lives," he nods and then adds, "Well, more drama anyway."

To wrap up our evening, the prancing pups need their walk. We gather leashes, treats, and poop bags before hitting the streets.

Descending our steps, I see Edna glaring at us from her porch. I shout, "Hiya neighbor!" and wave with my roll of poop bags. She does not see the humor and returns my wave with a scowl and a rude gesture.

"Is it my imagination or does she get more hateful each day?" Brad mutters as we walk away.

"Not your imagination. I feel like if she could start spitting venom at us, she would," the thought brings up a pit viper and it seems largely appropriate. "She's not winning neighbor of the year."

We pass by our friendlier neighbors and chat along the way. Each interaction restores why I love living in this community. The kindness and open warmth of the majority overrides the rudeness of the few. We even stop to say hello to the Avalons and Mr. Walters. Without Edna around, they're decently pleasant.

On the trip back around the block, we pass Gerald's house. I notice how much it has changed in the last month or so. He used to be so proud of his gardens, always outside weeding or watering. He called it 'puttering' and would spend hours each day. In the mornings and evenings, he would sit on the porch to relax. Now the house has a sad and closed up look to it. All the shades are drawn, the front and side yard in need of weeding. Gerald's favorite pineapple plant is dry as a bone and desperate for a solid watering.

"What is going on there?" I murmur mostly to myself.

"It's weird, huh? Like Gerald has locked himself in with his company," Brad responds to my musings.

"Yeah, his life seems to have come to a standstill. Maybe I should stop by tomorrow to check on him and make sure he's okay."

"I dunno honey. From the looks of it, they want privacy."

"I get it but something is off..." I continue, my concern for Gerald mounting.

"How did you say they're related?"

"I can't recall but maybe a cousin or nephew? I've never heard Gerald mention any family. It's seems weird that they're here now and staying with him."

"Hmmmm...sure does have a nice car though," Brad glances at the Bentley admiringly.

A moment of inspiration hits. "Why don't you stand next to it babe? I'll take your photo." Brad debates for a second but then moves in closer to the car. I snap a few photos. In each, I make sure the license plate is visible and easy to read.

"May I help you with something?" We both startle at the voice. The visitor from the porch stands off to the side of us. Despite his soft-spoken voice, his facial expression rivals cut marble.

"Oh! You scared us," I begin. "Apologies if we got too close to the car, it's so beautiful. Is it yours?"

"Yes, the car is mine," he responds, I hear the faint melodic tones of an eastern European accent or maybe the Baltics?

"It's a great car!" Brad chimes in, "We keep seeing it on the street and couldn't help but admire it. A Bentley isn't too common around here." He finishes with a smile and an appreciative glance back at the sleek dark gray car. Bless him for diving in!

"I feel awful that we haven't introduced ourselves yet, we like to welcome everyone to the neighborhood. Are you staying for good or just for a visit?" I probe gently for information.

"I am visiting my cousin temporarily. I am Patrick," he sticks out his hand stiffly. We return the introductions and shake hands. With nothing left to say, we wish him well and take our leave.

"Good save babe!" I whisper to Brad as we walk toward home.

"That was so awkward!" he exclaims, "I panicked, thought he was going to accuse us of spying on him."

"He thinks we're the goofy neighbors with dogs. Maybe it will work out in our favor." I get the feeling we're being watched. I whip out my phone and announce loudly, "Selfie time!"

We each hoist up a dog and I snap a photo, then adjust the angle and take a few more. Gerald's house is in the background. In the shadow of the porch, Patrick stands watching us. That same shiver runs up my spine again. Something is definitely not right there.

Once we're home, I text Chandra.

Me- *Pics from our walk tonight.* Followed by a heart-eyed emoji and two puppies. I attach two photos of Brad standing next to the car, and the selfie with Patrick staring at us. Seconds later, my phone dings.

Chandra- *OMG...these are great! Y'all so cute :)* with a string of emojis, including a high five.

Message received. She knows exactly why I've sent them. During our conversation yesterday, we agreed no texting about the case. Any communications should be in person, with meet ups arranged by phone or text.

Brad comes out to the porch with two cups of tea. He sees my lit-up phone and asks, "Chandra?" I nod and then show him the messages.

"I don't know if she can look up his license plate or find out more about him from the pictures," I bite at a hangnail on my thumb. An old stress habit from college. I keep picking at my nail, Patrick's face looms in my mind. A jab of pain and the sight of blood bring me back to the present. I tuck my finger against my palm to prevent further picking. "Don't you think it was creepy the way he watched us walk away?"

"It was. I'd prefer you stay away from him. Unfortunately, that means Gerald too."

I groan, "Come on, I just want to check on him."

"Then call him," Brad looks at me sternly. "I mean it."

He isn't one to give edicts or make rules. So, when he has a specific request like this, I am inclined to comply. Regardless of my feelings about it. I nod my head and promise to keep my distance.

Later that night, I find myself scrolling through the photos again. Zooming in on the selfie, I stare at the menacing glare on Patrick's icy face. In the corner of the photo, a brighter spot catches my eye. I zoom in even tighter. It's Gerald's face in the window. The photo is too pixelated to make out his expression. But I know without a doubt, it's him. Why didn't he come out to talk if he was right there? What's really going on in that house? The unknown gives me a desperate, panicky sensation deep in my core. Whether I have all the details or not, something is going on in that house.

I'll stick to my promise and only call. In the meantime, I pray that Chandra is able to find out some info. Either on Patrick or the car. She did warn she's switching to night shift for a few weeks, which can mean more or even less free time on her hands. Before switching off my light, I remind myself to be patient. We're all going to need it.

Chapter Eleven

Creeped Out

The buzz of my cell phone wakes me early on Saturday morning. I'm in the midst of a bizarre dream and it takes more than a second for the fog to clear. Chandra has sent a string of texts; her urgency grows with each message.

Weirdness happening here

OMG... We need to talk ASAP

Are you awake?!?

Never mind, it's early

Call me as soon as you wake up!!

What the heck?!? I scramble for my glasses before typing a response, otherwise it will end up as pure nonsense. Trying to be quiet leads to me knocking over my metal water bottle, last night's tea mug, and sending my phone crashing onto the floor. So much for subtlety. I doubt I could have made more noise if I'd tried. Brad sits bolt upright in bed with a "Huh, what?" combination.

"Sorry, sorry! I was trying to get my phone and glasses," I sigh, frustrated with my lack of coordination. "Go back to sleep, I'll go to the living room."

"Coffee?" he murmurs, his voice scratchy, and heavy with sleep.

"You got it babes," I kiss him on the forehead and cover him back up. Experience has proven, he'll be asleep in two seconds, but I'll start the coffee anyway. The dogs hop from their beds, and follow me into the kitchen, no doubt hoping it's breakfast time.

I let them out the back door, then return my attention to the phone.

I'm awake

What is going on?

Figuring I'd have a minute or two, I start filling the coffee pot with water from the tap. Lamenting having never figured out the automatic function. Although, I'd never intentionally get up before six o'clock on a weekend. My phone buzzes twice in rapid succession. Chandra's name is visible when I fish it out of my robe pocket.

Hey...don't text. Will call when I can

Not a good time

Okay, that's weird. She sent the nearly panicked string of texts that pried me out of bed at an ungodly hour on a Saturday morning.

And now, I can't text her? What in the world is going on? I take my frustration out on the coffee canister, prying the too tight metal lid free and aggressively scooping coffee into the back of the pot. Vintage is only cool when it cooperates. Otherwise, old metal tins with sticky lids just irritate. This morning I am ready to chuck it out the window.

Coco and Aggie are yipping in the yard, I rush to let them in. The last thing I need is Edna to hear them bark at this hour. She'll call in a noise complaint without hesitation. The pups rush in the door, blowing past me to huddle on the couch. They look terrified. The last time this happened, there was a coyote spotted in the neighborhood. I murmur reassurances to them and decide I should take a look. Because what woman in her jammies shouldn't go outside to check for threats?

I flick the lights on out back. Thankful for the additional spotlights Brad added last year. Fingers crossed that whatever it is will be scared off by the lights alone. There's a brief second, where I consider waking Brad to have him go with me. Instead, I grab a broom and go out to see if there's anything in the yard.

Brandishing the broom, I take up a position in the center of the yard, assuming this will give me the best vantage point. Straining my ears, the only sounds are the faint rustling of tiny critters. Nothing menacingly large, or thankfully human. After listening for a minute or so, I turn to head back inside. Midway across the lawn, I catch the motion lights turn on at Mirabel's.

This freezes me in place, had I missed something? The clattering sound of a trashcan crashing to the ground further down the street sends a shiver up my spine. I race toward the house. Sprinting through the doorway, I struggle to lock the screen and then sliding glass door. My heart is in my throat and my hands tremble violently. I'm shocked to feel tears prickling my eyes.

Coco and Aggie peer at me from the living room doorway, tails tucked, still clearly scared of whatever was out there. Once I've moved away from the door and am on the other side of the island, both race to me. Jumping frantically to be held. Their tiny shivering bodies crush me. I scoop them up and begin swaying back and forth. The motion soothing all of us.

"It scared me too lovies," I murmur into the tops of their fuzzy heads, holding them close against my chest.

No idea what was out there, but I am seriously praying it was a *what* and not a *who*. The thought of it being a person creeps me out and makes me sick to my stomach. While I am contemplating the horror of it having been a person lurking in the dark, the coffee beeps that it's done. Thankful for the distraction, I pour myself a cup. My trembling free hand makes it a challenging task and I slosh the coffee across the counter.

Today is not off to a stellar start. Chandra had better make up for it with news worthy of this mess.

As if I have conjured her with my thoughts, my cell phone buzzes from the puddle of coffee. I snatch it up and wipe it with a tea towel as I answer.

"This had better be worth it. My morning has gone to you-know-where in a handbasket."

"I have to be quick, so you need to listen, k?" Chandra harshly whispers.

I immediately snap to attention, a switch flips taking me from grumpy to dialed in, "You got it. Go."

"You were right, there's something off happening here. I don't think it's as simple as we thought though," Chandra takes a long pause. Her breathing is ragged, each exhale shakes slightly. I wonder if she's run to wherever she's calling me from. I hear voices in the background, they become louder, and I can tell they're walking past her. She resumes talking after they've faded out.

"I'm in the back hall by the stairwell." I make an uh-huh in agreement, having no concept of the department's internal layout, the description is unhelpful.

"I shared what we learned, and by that- I mean what you've learned, with Sergeant Lawrence. He had the most bizarre response. I could swear he knew all of this already."

"Didn't he tell you to look into it?" I'm trying to piece together our first conversation about the case. The lack of caffeine is impairing my memory. I could have sworn he did.

"Well...not exactly," she confesses, "He wasn't in opposition of me looking into it. Originally made a comment about things that might be connected. Then he let it drop. I took it as an opening to look into it."

"Oh geez," I grizzle, "That puts a way different spin on things."

"Sure does. Now hush, I've got more to get through," she inhales deeply and then launches into her next thought, "So I tell him what we've found and now suspect, including the description of the officer's voice. Not that I was expecting accolades, but at least a normal response. Instead, he gets stiff and quiet. Thanks me for 'looking so diligently into matters impacting our elderly community,'" Her voice is strident, betraying the depth of her emotion, "Those are his exact words. It was like a script being read."

"What kind of response is that?" I'm puzzled by his brush off. You'd think he would be glad she'd called it to his attention.

"No idea. He gathered up all of the papers and *took them* with him."

"Why'd he do that?"

"I tried to ask but he said so he can keep checking into things. There's only so much I can do; he's my supervisor's boss. Overstepping doesn't seem to be in my best interest. Officers can be terminated for insubordination."

"Point taken, but his response seems off."

"Exactly my thoughts. It led me to do some casual checking of my own overnight. There are more reports than we knew about from inside and outside of our precinct."

"Wait, how many?"

"You ready?" she pauses dramatically.

"Girlfriend, you better hustle, I haven't even had one cup of coffee yet..." I trail off, lifting my cup for a quick sip.

"At least fifty," she emphasizes the number, and then repeats, "fifty, as in five-oh." I spew the hot coffee back into the puddle on the counter. Nearly choking in the process. Hearing my sputtering, Chandra asks, "You okay?"

"I heard you, it's just that my brain can't quite wrap around this. Fifty cases? All similar circumstances?"

"Haven't had too much time to look, but on the surface, yes."

I gulp down an overly large drink of coffee and realize that I am in way over my head. Chandra is a trained law enforcement officer. I have a degree in marketing and used to make snazzy slide decks for a living. These two careers could not have less in common. Why am I involved again?

"Hey! You still with me?" Chandra whisper shouts. I can picture the *earth to Cici* look that she must have on her face.

"I'm here...trying to process what this means."

"Not sure yet myself, we can talk after I'm done at work. In the meantime, stay away from that creepy guy staying with your neighbor. The vibes are off in that situation. I can't find any reports based on the license plate or name, but from what you've told me, keep your distance."

My mind strays to the events of this morning. Could that be connected to Gerald's cousin? No way! Right? He certainly wouldn't be hanging out in the dark at my house. There's no reason for it.

"I don't mean to scare you," Chandra picks back up. She must have taken my silence for fear, instead of reflection.

"You didn't, I was just thinking about something from this morning," I start to tell her but then stop. What is there to tell? My dogs and I got scared in the dark, then a light came on down the street. For all I know, it could have been a cat or raccoon.

"Well, what is it?"

"Nothing, I'm undercaffeinated and was jolted awake this morning. Not in peak performance," I tease. This does the trick and seems to reassure her. We make plans to catch up after she gets some sleep and then disconnect.

During my conversation, the dogs have settled. I place them on the couch and walk to the kitchen to pour myself another coffee. Fifty cases, which is the lives of fifty people. Not just any people. These are vulnerable folks who need help. Whether I'm in over my head or not, I'm too involved. I hear the voice of Brad's grandmother reciting, 'in for a penny, in for a pound'. Guess this is where I am. At this stage, I am past the point of backing out. Time to get to work before this keeps happening.

Much later in the morning, Brad and I take the pups to the beach for a walk and playtime. Walking along in the hot sun, I relax and feel the stress and pressure of the early morning slip away. When I'd told Brad what happened, he freaked out (Brad style) and insisted we put up cameras this afternoon on the front, back, and side by the garage. I offered no argument. In the retelling of the story, I realized how genuinely terrifying it had been, for me and the dogs. I'd rather know we're all safe and be able to see who or what is outside.

Being near the water always soothes me. The noise in my brain clears with the sounds of gulls and waves. Brad's arms wrap around my waist, resting his chin on the top of my head. We stand watching the dogs clown around with seafoam and he chuckles. It is deep and rumbling, moving from his chest into my back. The sensation only adds to the peace and relaxation of the moment. I turn and kiss him, despite his eyes widening in surprise, he welcomes it. Brad isn't huge on public displays of affection but every now and then, spontaneity takes over.

"Thanks," I murmur with my lips pressed to his cheek. "I needed a morning with only you and the girls." He nods slowly. He knew. Of course, he knew. This man has loved me since we were teenagers. At this point, he knows me better than I know myself.

The dogs play until they drop to the sand with exhaustion. Salty, sandy, and happy. We each carry a sleepy little dog to the car. On the way home, we'll stop for cameras and supplies at the hardware store. Brad is anxious to get the cameras up today and has also added a doorbell camera to the list. He doesn't want me answering the door if I can't see who it is. I agree without hesitation. Plus, I'm such a nib nose, it will be fun to see all the goings on. And prevent sneak attacks from Edna. The last one may hold the most appeal for me.

While Brad shops, the pups and I grab coffees and pastries to go from Beans Eye View, a few shops over. Despite being soggy and sandy, they get plenty of love from the customers and staff. Which is their favorite part of any excursion.

In the shop, I flip through our community paper for date night ideas. An article on a new dry cleaner catches my eye. The article has a write-up on the business and a collection of pictures. In one of the photos, taking a customer's payment is the guy who took Francine's wallet! He doesn't simply look like him, I'm confident it is him. For a second I can't believe what I'm looking at. When it fully sinks in, I leap to my feet. Both dogs jumping to the ground, like we're under attack. They bark and growl ferociously, immediately on defense.

The suddenness has disrupted everyone around us. Customers stop eating and stare at me. Oh God.

"I...uh...so...sorry...got excited about an article in the paper...." I stammer. A flush creeping all the way to my hairline. I wave the crumpled paper in an attempt to prove I am, in fact, not in some sort of crisis. "Apologies for disrupting."

Embarrassed beyond words but too keyed up to really care. I hurry to collect our order, the dogs, and rush back to Brad. I run as fast as I can with my hands full. The crushed paper tucked into the back of my shorts. None of this is helping the scene I created in the coffee shop. I can only imagine all the people inside, watching me run away from the cafe.

"You're never going to believe this!" I shriek, running toward Brad. A panicked look crosses his face until he determines, I am simply excited and not being chased by a murderer.

In true solidarity, he is as thrilled as I am. We finally have a way to identify the thief! All because of a newspaper article. I snap a picture of the article, a close-up of his face, and the QR code for their website. Using the QR code, I visit their website, make a few notes, and grab screenshots. Did we just find a missing piece?

Chapter Twelve

Escalation

"Hmmm...it's a chain. Across most of southeastern Florida. Started in Miami in the early 2000s. Business owners are cousins; the employees are mostly family. They have a 'we're family- operated' thing going," I read snippets aloud to Brad.

"How many dry-cleaning shops do they have?"

"I see eight listed on the website and a coming soon announcement for Coral Gables."

"How in the world do they have that many family members available?"

"That...is a very valid point. Adding it to my list now," I jot down Brad's question. Eight, soon to be nine, spread across a portion of the state is a lot for a family to manage.

I open my messaging app and ask Chandra- *coffee later*?

She immediately replies- *you pick, I'll see you there!*

Pulling onto our street, the absence of the Bentley feels ominous. We've gotten so used to seeing it, that it now seems to belong on our quiet street. Seeming to read my mind, Brad says, "Too weird that the car is gone."

"Does he give you the heebie-jeebies?" I ask.

"Not sure if I'd called it that, but the dude is a weirdo. He stands and stares at everyone like we're all watching him. Makes me wonder if we should be..."

"Chandra told me his vibes are off and to keep my distance," I giggle at the use of vibes. Not a part of my typical vocabulary.

"His vibes are *off*," Brad says emphasizing the last word and smirking at me.

"Please don't ever say vibes again," I tell him with feigned horror. He laughs as he makes the turn into our drive. But his laughter is cut short, and he stops abruptly.

"Stay in the truck and call Chandra," he tells me as he jams the truck into park, jumping out his door and slamming it forcefully. Only then do I notice-our front window is broken. More than broken, it is shattered completely. Glass litters the porch and lawn. The entire plate glass window has been obliterated, leaving a gaping wound on the front of our home.

I rip my phone from the console and tap on Chandra's number.

"Pick up, pick up, pick up," I mutter while the phone rings. My fingers drumming furiously on the door handle.

"What am I picking up? Food or coffee?" Chandra answers jokingly.

"Chandra..." my voice breaking.

"I'm on my way, where are you?" she barks into the phone.

"We just got home, someone broke out our front window," I sob. The anxiety and fear of this morning returning in a rush.

"Is Brad with you?"

"He is. He made me stay in the truck with the dogs. He got out to look at the damage."

"Call him back over so I can talk with him," she tells me in a calm and direct voice. I do as she asks. Brad takes the phone from my outstretched hand and walks a few steps away. I can hear him talking quietly. The conversation mostly sounds like he's answering a series of rapid-fire questions. He snaps a few photos and returns to the truck.

"She wants me to wait in here with you. She said we need to 'preserve the crime scene'. Our home was referred to as a *crime scene*," his voice is tight and borderline angry. He takes my hand to comfort me. While gently stroking his thumb across the back of my hand, he takes a few deep yoga style breaths. It soothes both of us. "The police will be here soon. After we've spoken to them, we can go in. Chandra was very clear that you are not to say anything about investigating crimes."

"I understand. Pretty sure that would only cause trouble for her," I say and interlace my fingers with his. The dogs whine to be released from their seatbelts. Brad reaches back, unclipping the dogs with his other hand. His grip on mine is so strong, we're probably leaving fingermarks on one another. The dogs spring over the seat and into our laps. It's a moment of comic relief. They can't stand to be left out of any hugs or snuggles. Here we sit, the four us, all snuggled up and waiting for the police.

"We may have to rethink this," Brad says, sighing heavily. Before he can finish, a police cruiser and a purple Jeep screech to a halt in front of the house.

Chandra jumps from her car. Petite frame in leggings, a police department T-shirt, ball cap, and bulletproof vest. Gun in her hand. Two officers exit the squad car, a male and female. Also, in protective vests with weapons ready. Radios squawk loudly from people and vehicles. Chandra holds her hand up for us to wait.

The female officer from the squad car takes the lead and creeps toward the porch, her partner and Chandra in formation behind her. They approach the house, calling out, "Police!" and advising anyone in the home to exit with their hands up. No sounds from inside or outside the house. The doorknob turns easily, and the officers enter our home.

A sob escapes as I watch the trio stream in the front door. It all feels so invasive. Whatever it was this morning, now our home has been vandalized, and the police are searching each room of our tiny bungalow. Brad rubs my back and pulls me closer to him. I can feel his heart thudding; his breaths are sharp, and his body is tight. This has not been an easy day for him either.

The officer's sharp, "CLEAR!" rings out through the house. On exiting, she beckons us over.

"I'm Corporal Davies. This is Officer Hammond. We understand you are acquainted with Officer Boudreaux," she nods to each in turn and then points to a button-sized black object on her shirt front. I recognize it as a camera.

"A pleasure to meet you," Brad responds. "You are correct, we do know Officer Boudreaux."

"Perfect, can you walk me through the events of the day."

We explain pulling in the drive after running errands and Brad finding the window shattered. Then making the call to Chandra.

"Have there been any events or interactions with anyone lately that are a cause for concern?" she probes.

"Um," I don't know if I should proceed with the yard story or not. Brad gives me a reassuring nod. I relay the events of the morning, including the light turning on at Mirabel's and the trashcan banging farther down the street seconds later.

"Interesting that this occurred on the same day. We'll look into it and ask if any of the neighbors have camera footage," Corporal Davies says. I make a concerted effort not to look at Chandra. From the corner of my eye, I can see that she is not pleased. If you could picture displeasure as a painting, that would be her face. Brow furrowed, scowling. It's a look.

"I would recommend putting up some cameras," Officer Hammond advises.

Brad gives a mumbled agreement, then adds, "That's actually where we've come from. I picked up cameras for the property, and one with a doorbell. Would you have recommendations on where to place them?" With that the men walk off together to assess the property.

Corporal Davies clears her throat and looks pointedly at Chandra. Once she has her attention, in an overly loud voice, she says, "I'm going to speak with the neighbors. Why don't you assist Mrs. Larkin into her home?"

No need to go looking for them- Edna and her chums are standing across the street. Talking quietly and taking pictures. Can't wait for this to show up in the online neighborhood page.

Chandra simply nods and we turn to walk up the porch steps. She grabs me by the elbow and steers me past the broken glass. As the door closes, she leans in and whispers, "Where can we talk?"

I point to Brad's office off the living room, across from where we are standing. On the way by, I ask our smart speakers to play some classic rock with the assumption it will help drown out conversation. I saw it on a crime show once and hope it really works.

"What the heck was that all about?" I ask once we've closed the door. My eyes so wide, they feel like they're going to pop out of their sockets.

"Which part? Corporal Stepford Wife or the fact that you had a prowler and didn't tell me?" she replies angrily and swats at me with junk mail from Brad's desk.

"Well, I can explain the second half. You need to figure out the first one. I'd talked myself out of it this morning and then back into it. I'd planned to tell you over coffee."

"Was that why you texted me?"

"Oh my God, that's the best part!! And I totally forgot. I found HIM!"

"You found who?" she asks tersely. She's still annoyed and rightfully so.

"The dummy who took Francine's wallet. His picture is in the newspaper. Along with his name and where he works," I spout triumphantly. Chandra stares at me dumbfounded. "That's pretty much what my face looked like earlier too."

"Show me," she says. I grab the crumpled newspaper and my phone from my bag.

"Right here. His name is Stefan Markovic. Works at PK Brothers Dry Cleaning and More. They opened a new franchise in town a couple of months ago."

"Can I have this?" she reaches for the newspaper in my hand. I willingly hand it over, despite my excitement over the photo, I am more than ready to give this whole thing over to Chandra.

Chapter Thirteen

Shattered

When Chandra was here, it was easier to put on a facade of bravery. The moment she left, heavy, hot tears began to fall and have barely stopped. Each glance at the front window wrecks me. Seeing the dark gaping hole felt like a physical wound. Brad had covered the opening with a sheet of plastic and tape. But it still felt too exposed. His friends, Paul and Micah, came over and helped him mount the cameras and doorbell. By the time all were installed and set up, it was well after 10 p.m.

He collapses onto the couch next to me with a loud sigh. One of the sighs that comes from deep inside, like it was drawn up from the well of your soul. I pat my shoulder and he tips onto me, calling an extended 'timber' as he falls over. We both laugh softly, trying to find what humor we can. Sensing an opportunity to snuggle, Coco and Aggie rush to join us. Each twirling and dancing to kiss our faces,

Brad's salty with sweat and mine with tears. Brad encircles us all in a hug and the dogs settle in.

"You okay?" Brad asks, his chin resting on the top of my head. I note the tightness of his posture, his pounding heart, his fingertips press firmly into the backs of my arms. Knowing this wasn't a relaxing ending to the beautiful morning we started out with.

"I will be, are you?" turning my face to rest against his neck. I breathe in deeply, the tang of his sweat, mixed with deodorant and remnants of cologne is comforting. He nods slowly in response, pressing his face into my hair. The longer we sit, the calmer we become. Our thudding hearts slow and our breaths synchronize. So we sit, two tiny dogs snuggled between us, oblivious to the turmoil of the day. Their happiness in the moment relaxes me further. My eyes rest on the destroyed front window but tears no longer fall.

"You're getting there, huh?" Brad gently asks.

"Yeah. It is what it is. Crying isn't changing anything."

"You don't have to be okay with this..." he says, turning to watch me. Concern written across his handsome face.

"I know, but I also realize that staring and weeping won't do either of us any favors. I genuinely am working my way through it."

One of my other fatals is insisting that I am always fine. No matter what it is. I come from generations of women who keep going. It's what we do. Brad loves that internal fierceness but also encourages me to feel what my actual emotions are instead of what I should do. *I don't do that*, I think and chuckle out loud. Brad turns to face me and smirks. I smile, silently thanking him. He leans and kisses my forehead. Then he rests his face against mine and sighs loudly, turning it into a groan. He's accepting it in his own way.

Before long, I realize I can barely keep my eyes open. Brad's head is tipped back on the couch, eyes closed, mouth slightly gaped open. The dogs are curled in his lap and all are snoring softly. They alternate grumbling and squeaking sounds. I whisper, "To bed?" Brad murmurs his agreement, and we carry the dogs to our bedroom. A soft click of the door, and I immediately feel secure in our bubble.

Morning dawns, with a violent rainstorm. Booming thunder rattles our bedroom windows, and I rocket from bed, completely disoriented. My first thought is that the plastic won't hold. I attempt to grab clothing that will make me semi-presentable but require minimum time to put on. Whipping the bedroom door open, I dash for the porch. Wrapping my hand around the handle is the pause I need for my brain to catch up. The front window (or what's left of it) is now protected by a large sheet of plywood. I mutter, "What in the blazes?" while opening the door fully.

Brad stands in the yard, soggy in a rain slicker. The hood is pushed back, and his hazel eyes are sparkling with delight. He takes a few steps toward the porch, lifting a lidded cup my way.

"Nice outfit babe," he gestures at my clothes. Only then do I really look at what I've thrown on. Brad's sweats, which are about three sizes too big, and a ratty T-shirt from my old job, emblazoned with *Howlan's Dream Team* in a garish font. I've completed the outfit with a pair of sparkly neon pink flip-flops. I give him a twirl while he shouts an extended 'woo' from the yard and claps. With a final curtsy, I turn to head in the doorway. Pounding footsteps rush up the stairs and I am lifted into the air. Brad's cold, wet jacket soaks the back of my shirt as he engulfs me in a bear hug. Both of us are cackling as he carries me into the house, leaving a trail of rainwater in his path.

One piping hot shower later, we are seated in the kitchen while coffee brews. This morning feels like a gift, despite the large hole in our house, I have Brad home for the second day in a row. He gets up to pour our coffee, and I grab burritos from the freezer to reheat. A part of me forgets why he's home and savors the sweetness of our extra morning.

"I'll have meetings in the afternoon, but the first part of the day is all for us," he tells me between sips of coffee. I cradle my mug in both hands and blow across the top. My brain begins sifting through all the fun things we could do with a few free hours. These dreams come crashing down when Brad continues, "It would be a good idea if we called the insurance company for their contractors list and then made inquiries for estimates."

I cannot think of a less exciting way to spend the morning. Still, I nod in agreement. It has to get done, and of the two of us, Brad is better at this stuff. With a forlorn sigh, I mumble an "okay," and then grab the burritos from the toaster oven. Sensing my disappointment, he suggests, "We can go to Azúcar for lunch?"

This does the trick and restores my good mood. I am a sucker for lunch with him, especially when the food is a guaranteed hit. I munch away happily on my burrito, the crispy tortilla and melty cheese are a winning combo.

"There's something else we should talk about this morning," Brad says. His voice is tight, almost as if he's nervous or uncomfortable. Without knowing the reason, I become immediately nervous and give him a go-on gesture.

"Last night, I put a lot of thought into this situation. You started out helping from the goodness of your heart. But with this-" he gestures to the window, "I just don't know if you helping Chandra is the best idea." His cheeks have reddened, and he most definitely looks uncomfortable now.

"Are you asking or telling me to quit?" I spit out. The words come out with a high-pitched squeak at the end.

"Honey, I am not telling you anything. I am asking you, do you think this is wise?" Again, he turns to look at the window. A deep furrow between his brows and the set of his jaw show me how much this has gotten under his skin.

"It could be unrelated..." I offer weakly, knowing full well that is not likely.

"There's a slim chance, I'll give you that. Between the weird neighbor, who's always staring at us, the missing items, and vandalism, I think it is time to let the police handle it," he raises his hand to halt my next sentence, "I know that what you're doing matters. But with the escalation, please leave it to the professionals."

I sit and stare at him. I cannot believe he wants me to stop. The images of the crime victims play in my mind like a movie. Then the crippling fear from last night pours in. While I don't want to back out, I understand his concern. He does have my safety in mind, probably more than I do. Is it possible for me to stop now? I can call Chandra and give her a heads-up. For the moment, I promise to think it over and let him know by dinnertime. This seems to make him feel better, at least a little bit. Some of the tension leaves his face. I wouldn't describe him as relaxed, but enough that we carry on with breakfast without strained silence.

Most of the morning is spent on the phone. Three hours later, we finish calls with the insurance company. It was a series of long, dry, anxiety inducing conversations. Midway through I said a short prayer of thanks that Brad took this task. I would have given up an hour in. Two contractors are scheduled to come tomorrow and give estimates. I assure Brad I won't sign anything until he's looked it over. Paperwork is NOT my strong suit. I've signed us up for countless things that require fees to get out of. I know my limits, finally. The last one was a doozy!

Chapter Fourteen

Things Get Serious

Pulling up in front of the cafe, I gasp. Brad whips his head around and I point. A purple Jeep is parked up the street.

"Chandra is here. Wonder why?" I say with a girlish giggle. "I hope she's here to see Seb."

"The infamous Seb works here?" Brad says wide-eyed, and as excited as I am. My husband is committed to girl gossip. He's been given the full scoop on things. "Hurry! What if she leaves *before* we get there?"

Brad launches from the truck, eager to see if Chandra and Seb are in the cafe. He gives a hurry-up motion with his hand. I am struggling with my purse, putting on lipstick, and sliding my sandals into place. It takes me far too long, but I finally make it out of the truck and Brad closes my door for me. Holding hands, we half-jog across the street. He swings the door wide for me to go ahead of him.

Craning our necks as we enter, we try to sneak a peek of the cute new couple.

Wren swoops up to our table with two waters and a small plate of hot, crispy chicharron- one of Brad's favorites. She gives a chipper, "Be back in a sec!" and then floats off to another table.

Brad whispers a quiet, "Oh yeah!" before breaking off a section. He crunches happily while I take a moment to glance around. I take in all the tables, looking for two familiar faces. She's got to be here, right?

As I'm about to call it a lost cause, I hear Chandra's laugh. Loud and clear. She's got one of those laughs you can pick out in a crowd. It's deep but melodic, often making others smile or join in- even if they don't know what's funny.

Got her!

Five tables up toward the patio, her hair threw me off. Yesterday, she'd worn it long, sleek, and midway down her back. Today, it is a round and full head of curls. I squeak with happiness when I lay eyes on her tablemate. Seb. He leans back in his chair, relaxed and laughing. White teeth gleaming, eyes sparkling. He is clearly enjoying their date.

Brad whips his head around, eyes alight. He can tell I've spotted them. I tap him to draw his attention. Keeping my hand low on the table to avoid being obvious, I point to their table. His face transforms from puzzled to delighted in a split second. He follows my lead and keeps his gestures small giving a mini fist pump at his side.

I slide my phone out and send Chandra a text- *how's the date going?*

We watch for a reaction. Who knows if she'll even check her phone? She is on a date after all. I see her glance at her wrist and then a slight shaking of her shoulders.

My phone dings- *stalker*

I burst out laughing and see her spin around. She grins and throws me a wink. Leaning toward Seb, she shows him the message. His turn to search for us. When he finds us in the crowded cafe, Brad and I wave in unison. Prompting a round of laughs from both tables.

Another small ding- *join us?*

I quickly tap- *Nah, enjoy the date* with a crown and sparkly heart emoji.

She's fast on the response- *your loss, my gain* with a winky face and a series of hearts.

Wren reappears, ready for us to order. I've been so invested in my shenanigans that I haven't even looked. Thankfully, Wren kicks off with the specials. She's reciting them with enough enthusiasm that you'd think she'd made each one. My stomach growls when she mentions a Ropa Vieja sandwich, a new item to the cafe.

"I'm guessing that one sounded the best?" she says with a smirk. I nod with perhaps too much vigor, but I'm too hungry to be ashamed. She taps in my order and a traditional Cuban for Brad. For good measure, we add two Coladas. We can never have too much coffee. Wren wheels away from the table and Brad asks, "We sharing?" a hopeful lilt at the end of his question,

"Hmmm..." I murmur, squinting at him. He makes puppy dog eyes at me and flutters his lashes dramatically. "Just because you're cute," I tell him and he blows me a kiss, looking very pleased with himself. "Don't make me take it back..." He harrumphs and takes the last chicharron, popping it in his mouth, crunching loudly.

When the food arrives, we split up the sandwiches evenly. The grilled crust is crisp, the bread is chewy and soft. I start with the Ropa Vieja. Both sandwiches are piled with meat, served with black beans, rice, and sweet plantains.

"Oh my lord," I mumble around my huge bite. The buttery texture and savory flavor of the meat make me follow up with a happy dance. They've struck gold with this one. Brad drops the Cuban he was about to start with. He grabs his half of the Ropa Vieja and takes a large bite. His eyes widen as he slowly chews, enjoying himself thoroughly. In moments like this, I have no idea how he tolerates my cooking. The man LOVES food. He nods his head and wipes his mouth.

"Whatcha think?" a chipper voice pipes up. Wren has swung back to our table. "I could hear you two from over there," she points to a few tables away and giggles. My face reddens knowing others have heard too. I shrink behind my napkin in embarrassment. She explains the sandwich was her idea and she was thrilled to hear how much we enjoyed it. We gush over how delicious it was and she beams with pride. While we chat about the merits, she shares how the idea came to life. Freshly baked bread, leftovers in the fridge, and ravenous hunger after a skating event. After that, she'd make them on her break at the cafe. The kitchen staff sampled her creation and decided to add her sandwich to the menu rotation.

While we're chatting, Chandra and Seb drop into chairs at our table. Chandra snags a plantain from my plate, I glower and hold my remaining bite of the sandwich out of her reach. She grins and happily chews her stolen treat.

After swallowing, she says, "Must be good, I heard y'all moaning from our table." My embarrassment returns full throttle. She laughs and says, "Kidding! I overheard you raving about the sandwich as we walked up." I swat at her with my napkin and stick out my tongue.

Seb orders another round of coffee and guava and cheese-stuffed pastries. Chandra rubs her hands together and licks her lips. Seb smiles and says, "Perks of dating the owner."

I break out into a grin, my smile so wide it makes my face hurt. "Is it official now?"

"As of this lunch date it is," Chandra confesses. Her voice a little giddy and a blush on her cheeks. Seb reaches for her hand and gives it a sweet squeeze. Brad and I coo an 'aww' at their new couple cuteness. Chandra is too distracted to even react. She's only got eyes for Seb at this moment.

Once they've broken off their eye-batting, Chandra asks how we're feeling after the events last night. We give a run down of all the insurance fun we'd had earlier but sum it with, "We're okay." She frowns and leans forward, not believing a word of our assurances.

"We got to work on it after we left last night," she begins cautiously while looking around the room. After reassuring herself that no one was in earshot, she continues, "I updated Sarge on the vandalism and the article you showed me. He wants me to express his 'sorrow of the criminal actions but gratitude that you were not harmed.' His exact words, he was very formal. Mostly because I had to confess more of your involvement and I'm pretty sure he's mad."

"How'd you know he was mad? Getting the ol' silent treatment?" I offer, unfazed that he knows. Maybe it will protect us?

"Quite the opposite, he yelled at me for fifteen minutes."

"Good grief!" I sputter. "Does this mean I'm off the case?" My voice tinged with apprehension and a small amount of relief.

"You'd think! He ended with now that I've drug you in this far, I may as well see how else you can help," her eyes flick back and forth from me to Brad. His face is tense, jaw set. I pull up our conversation and his concerns for my safety. I swallow around the lump forming in my throat. His expression reveals his internal conflict.

He takes a slow deep breath and asks, "Can you promise she'll be safe?"

He stares directly at Chandra, waiting for her response. To her credit, she stares back without so much as a twitch or blink. Chandra nods slowly.

"I'll do everything I can to keep her safe," she finally answers. My eyes are bouncing back and forth. The tension at our table is as thick as the humidity outside. Brad nods his head. I breathe in sharply, nervous to exhale. Does he mean it?

"That's the best I can ask for," he says, and face relaxes some. Not fully, but some. Chandra responds with a smile and fist bump. I squirm in my seat, a mixture of relief and excitement.

"For the record, I could have made my own choice," I chime in. They turn my way and say, "Sure" in unison.

Half-irritated, I respond with a clipped, "Good." Then lean back and cross my arms, attempting a tough expression. Unlike their staring contest, I cave under their stares.

Seb provides a helpful distraction, "Now that we've gotten that over with, how about dessert?" None of us noticed the coffee and pastries that have silently appeared on the table. He gestures for us to dig in. Despite feeling full from lunch, I begin devouring mine.

After we've annihilated every crumb, we decide it's time to wrap up. Brad has an afternoon of meetings. The first starting within the next hour. The guys shake hands. Chandra leans in to hug me, whispering hurriedly, "Call me later. I have an idea!"

Chapter Fifteen

How Could He Say No?

A stakeout? Me on a stakeout? That's all I can think when Chandra proposes the idea. Seems preposterous but at the same time it doesn't.

What better duo to make this happen? I live on the same street which means my car won't be noticed if it's parked anywhere on the block. The biggest hurdle will be convincing Brad that this is a good plan. I know he'll have a hundred questions considering he only came back on board yesterday. My brain feels like a tornado, swirling with all the questions I have, combining with the questions I'm guessing Brad will throw out. I've been stressing all morning.

The best time to bring up any big request is always after a good meal. The bigger, the better. I hit the internet to find some dinner options. Wowing with a homemade meal is always a win. This is one I can't mess up.

I go back to how much Brad loved the dinner Mirabel helped me put together, he talked about it for days. It's been well over a month, fingers crossed that I get it right. Now to remember what all it was. After wracking my brain and checking my phone, I cave and call Mirabel. Going straight to the source feels like a better plan.

"My lovely Cici!" Mirabel says as a greeting. Her voice is soothing and bright. Like sunshine. She always makes me miss my grandmother; it warms my heart whenever we're together.

"Is all well?" she sweetly asks, knowing there must be a reason for the call. I usually just pop by on walks with the pups.

"I need help," I begin and then explain I need to cook an amazing dinner to sway Brad on a big ask.

"Claro, claro. The way to a man's heart is through his stomach. I know just what to do, can you come over?"

"You're a lifesaver!" I exclaim. She asks me to give her thirty minutes and come over. I'll use the time to put together a small gift to thank her.

I knock on her side door and turn the handle to enter. Mirabel has a family policy. If you're family by blood or her choice, the rules apply. Knock once and then come in. I've tried to discourage her from leaving the door unlocked. But she considers it an act of love to make her home available to family and friends.

"Cici!" a booming male voice calls out. Alfie pops his head around from the living room. His wife, Elena, joins him. Both wave excitedly and beckon me in. There's a part of me that feels I should be embarrassed for needing help with dinner. Instead, I am happy to see my friends. A round of hugs and catching up follows. I haven't seen Elena in weeks. She rocks me back and forth in a bear hug, reminding me so much of my Aunt Lora.

"My sweet girl," Mirabel wraps me in a hug, leaning back she pats my face, "You're getting too thin. We must fix this." Taking me by the hand, we walk down the short hall to the kitchen. It's a sunny yellow, with lemons and ivy decorating the walls and unused space. She loves a theme. Her outfit coordinates with the kitchen. Her tangerine glasses match perfectly. She's wearing a white tunic with large citrus fruits over white capris.

The smell of roasting meat makes my mouth water. Elena opens the oven and waves her hand to waft the scent in my direction. Weak in the knees, I nearly float forward. A loud growl erupts from my stomach. I wrap both arms around my waist and giggle, embarrassed that my stomach gave me away.

"See? I knew you needed to put meat on those bones," Mirabel leans to me and crooks a finger, I bend down to be closer. "Would you like to know the plan?" she whispers. I nod so vigorously; it makes me dizzy momentarily.

"Elena and I are making roast pork to keep on hand, not for dinner tonight." Mirabel begins and I stare open-mouthed, thinking *who makes food to have as an extra?!?* My boggled mind is brought back by Mirabel, "It won't be ready until after four. Can you come pick some up or do you need Alfie to drop it off?"

"Mirabel! That is too much. I couldn't possibly..." I sputter. She cuts me off by holding her hand, emphasizing her point she shakes her head back and forth.

"No! No! No! You must. We insist. I know what you've been up to. Desmond filled me in a few days ago. Whatever you need to ask Brad must be important and I assume relates to our friends. Correct?"

"Yes! Chandra wants me to keep helping and it might be dangerous. I need to have Brad on my side for this. Otherwise, I don't think I can keep going. If he's not in, I can't do it on my own."

"You are never alone. You have many supporting you and the best one," she gestures to the ceiling with her eyes raised. "But I do know what you mean, Brad is your other half. You've come to rely on him. It's natural. We'll do whatever we can to help."

"Sit, let's plan your side dishes," Elena beckons me to the table in the breakfast nook.

Walking the few steps, I begin to sniffle. Now is not a time for tears. I can feel the support from Mirabel and her family. My heart burns in my chest and I suddenly feel undeserving. What if I fail? What if I can't help the way I want to? I take a small, shuddering breath. Then I feel a small hand and frail arm wrap around my waist.

"Come, we've got work to do," Mirabel moves me forward into the chair Alfie has pulled out. Elena is seated with a paper and pencil, ready to get the plan in place.

Alfie delivers the pork at quarter past four. The smell is absolutely heavenly, and my mouth begins watering. Meaty and savory with a hint of sweetness from the citrus. There's no way I am going to pass this off as a meal I made. I thank him profusely as he hands off the large tinfoil pan.

"It's nothing! We do for family," he waves away the thanks and smiles genuinely. He blows a kiss and rushes off the porch, calling over his shoulder, "Hope all goes well!"

Brad opens the front door and inhales deeply. I hear a growling groan, "What is that smell?"

Two quick thunks tell me he's kicked his shoes off and is headed to the kitchen. With perfect timing, I twirl to face him. A plate piled with roast pork, rice, black beans, and sweet plantains. Brad's eyes widen as he reaches for the plate, fingers waggling for me to hurry. With a giggle, I pass it off and shoo him to the lanai.

I follow behind quickly with my plate and am delighted to see Brad waving the aroma to his face. He sees me and breaks into a huge smile.

"Hungry?" I ask with a sly smile.

"I didn't think I was until I smelled this," he answers and digs his fork into the pile of steaming pork, a hunk of warm bread in the other hand.

I forgot to mention the bread- purchased from the bakery up the street. All I had to do was warm the loaf in the oven. Easy peasy! Staring at my own plate, I can't take it anymore and dive in. Opting to go for the bean/plantain combo first. Sighing heavily and enjoying the flavors of each.

In moments, Brad's plate is empty and he's mopping up the remaining bits with bread. After his final swipe, I offer a second helping. He nods his head so briskly, I'm afraid he'll injure himself. When he passes the plate to me, he swats me on the backside and laughs. Clearly, the food is doing the trick.

We wrap up dinner and I bring out decaf coffee and a homemade (by me!) coconut cream pie. Brad's eyes are the size of saucers. He helps me sit all the items on the table, sliding his pie as close as he can get it.

Before scooping up his first bite, he looks up at me. In sync, we hold up our forks like battle weapons and then stab into the pie. It is silky, cold, and perfectly creamy. The toasted coconut provides a contrasting crunch. A delicious, sweet ending to our heavy meal.

While finishing the dishes, Brad says, "Out with it," and leans to make eye contact.

"I am shocked by your assumption!" feigning offense, I continue, "why can't I make you a special dinner?"

"It's a random Wednesday, no special events, and this was a lot of effort. I enjoyed every single bite, but..." he trails, pointing to the leftovers and stack of clean dishes.

"Busted, huh?" I sheepishly ask. He nods, appearing pleased. Now or never, "I need to ask you something." My voice is halting and suddenly my throat feels tight with anxiety. Brad shifts and leans back against the counter. I may as well get it over with. Beating around the bush isn't going to make it any different.

"Chandra has asked me to go on an unofficial stakeout with her," I blurt.

"I'm sorry, did you say a *stakeout*?" Brad repeats, his brow furrowed.

"Yeah," losing steam, I exhale the huge breath I've been holding and fling the damp dish sponge into the empty sink. "You're going to say no, aren't you?" Tears sting my eyes, and I can't turn to face him. I know he won't want me to and I can't bare the disappointment.

"Not necessarily. Tell me more about it," Brad says and moves to stand closer.

"Really?" excitement and relief flood through me. I spin around to face him. "What do you need to know?"

"The plan would be a good place to start," he says with a smirk. I nod and then reach for coffee cups. We'll need a quick cup to map this out.

I am getting the cream from the fridge when I hear clinking. Brad is topping each mug with a bit of whiskey. He beckons to follow him onto the lanai with a nod. Squealing quietly, I grab my notebook and phone, practically skipping after him through the doorway. Coco and Aggie dancing in my wake. I can't wait to show him what we've planned. In a stroke of rare focus, I'd mapped it out and included answers to questions I thought he may have.

Chapter Sixteen

Stakeouts with Girlfriends

Chandra answers on the first ring, blurting, "What'd he say?"

"YES! He said yes!" I shout, literally shout. Despite being shy of 8 a.m. I dance around the kitchen to celebrate. My energy is through the roof this morning.

"No way! I could have sworn he'd axe this plan."

"You and me both sister," I laugh and take a loud slurp of my hot coffee.

"We need to get on this, when are you free?" Chandra asks, the sound of rustling pages in the background.

After comparing calendars (the paper kind), we settle on tonight after dinner. She'll come here to eat, making it more natural for her car to be on the block. At dinner, we'll finalize the details to allay

Brad's remaining safety concerns. She even offers to bring dinner as a thank you. I happily agree and we end the call. Both of us are feeling ten feet tall this morning.

As promised, the doorbell rings at six. Brad opens the door and welcomes Chandra in. I'm setting the table as she sets a large pot in the center, Brad follows with two smaller dishes.

"Not so much on the simple dinner?" I tease.

"My mama didn't raise a fool. Showing appreciation with food is one of my favorites," Chandra answers with a smile and shake of her head.

"It's one of my favorite ways to be thanked," Brad chimes in, returning with a cold bottle of white wine. We nod and move the glasses toward him. We've got HOURS to go before the stakeout kicks off. May as well enjoy ourselves. Brad pours and Chandra dishes out red beans and rice, sliced grilled sausage, and spoonbread. When that smell hits, we all inhale deeply and snatch up our spoons. Aggie and Coco whine from their spots on the chaise. They'll be lucky if there are any leftovers or nibbles to share.

Just before midnight, Chandra and I sneak out the backdoor, threading our way between the fences. We're dressed in black workout gear and running shoes. In the event someone asks what we're doing, we've decided that it will be going to or coming from a workout depending on the time. I've left my Jeep unlocked and turned off the interior lights. Moving slowly to avoid excessive noise, each of us slide into the front seat and softly close our doors. Chandra gives me an *okay* hand signal, pinching her thumb and index finger into a small circle. I reciprocate with a thumbs up. Since my Jeep has a soft top, we'd opted to keep conversation to a minimum. We aren't quite sure how far the sound will travel.

Chandra opens the bag at her feet and withdraws a small camera, night vision goggles, a pen and notebook, and her cell phone. I'm not going to lie, surprised that she's been able to cram all of that into her little bag. Pretty sure she also has a gun in there, but I am not asking. With a nod, I grunt with approval. She winks and hands me the notebook and pen. I see a couple of instructions written, mostly about timestamping. I mark my spot with the pen and tuck the notebook above the visor.

Leaning behind me, I pull out a thermos and two small mugs from a tote on the back seat. The smell of coffee is an instant mood booster. My anxiety over the situation is temporarily replaced with joy over a hot cup of coffee. Chandra pumps her first and reaches for the offered cup. We find comfy spots in our seats and raise our mugs in solidarity. Our shared excitement bubbles over and we grin at one another. Is this not the best girls' night out or what?

We'd selected a spot down across the street and three doors down from Gerald's. Brad had moved my car mid-afternoon; he'd planned a garage cleanout to give more credibility. Having to do the drive-way shuffle is not uncommon on our street. Tight driveways with single-car garages behind the houses don't leave much room for company. Plus, half the neighbors near us know what is going on. I saw Desmond move his car out in front of mine. Later Alfie moved his mother's humongous vintage Caddy out in front of that. Both drug projects out into their empty driveways to fill in the space and act as distractions. We appreciated the extra cover the cars provided.

Gerald's house is quiet with the lights off for the first couple of hours. Shortly after two o'clock, a light flicks on in the base-ment. We can't see inside, but the light from the small glass block windows shines onto the foundations of the houses on either side. The sparkling shapes are disorienting and prevent a clear count of occupants. Chandra snaps to attention and points at the notebook I tucked in the visor. I quickly open to the marked page and note the time on my cell phone. Throwing my phone into the console, I lean for a better view. A hand presses into my shoulder and Chandra shakes her head, pushing back slightly on me. Point taken, don't be too obvious. You know when someone says, 'don't look' what do you automatically do? You physically cannot stop yourself.

I'm dying to see what is happening. It makes me twitchy, and I start to drum my nails, my go-to tune is a song from a childhood cartoon. Chandra turns to me with *are you serious?* written all over her face. The drumming stops and I choose to chew the end of the pen to release my energy. She sighs and goes back to watching the house intently. Her entire body is rigid, ready for action. I do my best to mimic her posture and calmness. Not an easy task. I soon find myself slumping back into the driver's seat.

We watch for another thirty minutes before a dark SUV glides into the empty driveway. I note the time and what I can see of the license plate. Only the first three letters and last number are clear enough to read from this distance. Chandra snaps a series of rapid-fire photos, with the camera resting on the doorframe. I exhale a shuddering breath through pursed lips. I'm afraid to move and disturb the scene unfolding in front of us.

This feels momentous, we might actually see something valuable tonight. Chandra's breathing has picked up pace as well, I know she's feeling it too. A short man in a black tracksuit exits the passenger side of the vehicle. He glances around quickly, I guess to make sure all is quiet on the street. I'm not a criminal so I'm just spit balling here on his motives. Seems like what a shady criminal would do. He gives a sharp nod to the driver and then rounds the back of the house, disappearing from view. The driver remains in the running vehicle.

At this point, I realize I have been holding my breath and I'm a little dizzy. Chandra gives me a thumbs up without turning from the window. I use the moment to take a few of those slow breaths that are supposed to center you. Wouldn't describe myself as that but I do feel less lightheaded.

A light in the back of the house comes on, shadows dance along the fence. The man is talking to another person inside Gerald's house. From this distance, none of the words are audible. Only the hushed rumbles of voices in the quiet night. Another light comes on the front of the house and the basement lights go out. Assuming they've got a routine down if this has been going on for most of the last year. Heavy curtains on the windows prevent all but cracks of light from escaping. We can see movement as the light changes when the occupants walk back and forth by the windows. Guarantee whatever we aren't supposed to see is split between the basement and front rooms. Gerald's house is laid out similarly to Linda's. The dining room is on the left, next to Desmond's house and the living room is on the right, next to Mirabel's. I make a note of the group's progress and assembling in the dining room.

Chandra clicks a few more photos of the house, lights, and car. Her camera is aimed at the car when I see the curtains shift slightly. The panels split open wide enough to see a section of face peering out. They tightly close a second later. I gasp and poke Chandra on the arm. When she moves the camera back, the house lights go out. All of the lights, in one motion. I swing my head to check the other

155

houses on the street, was there a power outage? *Please* be a power outage. Instead, houses up and down the block have small lights on in different windows. What used to be comforting now ramps my nerves up. A chilly panic runs through me, they know we're here...

I do my best to visualize the face, male with heavy, dark brows and glasses. Using all that the quick glimpse gave me. I can't fully describe the face, but I know one thing- it isn't Gerald. He is taller, with white hair and brows, no glasses. Was it my imagination or did he look right at us? Could he have seen us in the car? My mind and heart are racing. Chandra puts her hand on my forearm and makes a slow down motion with her hand. One of those palm to the floor and push it down type. She's telling me to stay calm. I make a tiny tight nod, almost imperceptible, and do my best to relax.

Time seems to stand still. We sit in silence, our breathing and my heart thudding in my ears are the only sounds. An hour after he's arrived, we see the small man exit. He carries two duffle bags, each bursting at the seams, and a tattered cardboard box. Walking to the back of the SUV, he opens the liftgate. Chandra snaps photos of him and the boxes filling the back. Without any hesitation, or concern of being watched, he places all three items in the back and softly closes the door. Once he is in the vehicle, it backs out with the lights off. I watch them exit our street and into the main neighborhood. Turning once again to Gerald's house, I see the curtains in the living room are now open an inch or so. Chandra swings her camera and nods to me. She takes a few quick photos. I point to the second floor and see the hallway curtains are now cracked open as well. All the proof we need, they've definitely been watching.

The question is- was it us or their visitors?

Chapter Seventeen

Noted

Dawn is nearly here. Chandra gives me the signal. It's time to go. Earlier we'd decided to make our escape before the sun rises.

Walking briskly to my house, we take turns looking at and past one another. Each attempting to keep an eye on our surroundings. No lights, no movement, no one seems to be awake on the street. Entering the house, we take a collective sigh of relief. Leaning against the door, I think I've never been happier to be in my own home. Heart pounding, hands shaking, I do not think I am built for stakeouts after all. I silently scream while jumping up and down. There's too much energy and it needs to be released somehow.

"Coffee?" Brad asks from the kitchen. His soft baritone a comfort. I rush into the kitchen and wrap him in a tight hug. "I'm taking that as a yes," he says and kisses me on the forehead. I cling to him like a baby sloth while he moves around making the coffee. My shuffling steps match his larger ones.

Chandra has dropped onto the couch, curled up with a dog tucked on either side. "I'll take a cup," she says, her voice thick with exhaustion and hours of silence.

Over coffee we share what we saw with Brad. His concern grows when I mention the face in the curtains. It gave me the creeps and he can tell how rattled I am. Putting a protective arm around me, he draws me close. His heart is thudding against me.

"You're sure it wasn't Gerald?" he finally asks.

"Without a doubt, the face was too young, and he had glasses on. Remember when Gerald got his cataract surgery? He stopped wearing glasses and was so proud of himself that he donated his collection." Brad nods his head, calling up the memory of Gerald showing us all the glasses he was dropping off at the Lions Club. I shiver thinking of the face in the curtains, looking right at us.

"We got a lot," Chandra murmurs, she's reviewing all the images on her camera. "I'll upload these and share my progress with Sergeant Lawrence this afternoon. I'm on the late shift, so I can organize them before submitting. I'll need your notes too."

I groan, remembering that I'd left the notebook in the Jeep. Safely tucked in the visor. Right where I'd left it when getting out. My brain said *leave it somewhere safe*. Brad chuckles, pretty sure he saw that coming. He stands up and grabs the keys.

"Back in a sec," he says over his shoulder. I throw an air kiss at his retreating back. Chandra and I resume our quiet coffee consumption, happy to spread out and relax. Savoring the freedom of the living room.

The front door bangs open, crashing into the wall.

"Babe!" Brad shouts as he races through the doorway, into the living room.

I jump up and spill coffee all over myself and the rug. He turns flush-faced with his chest heaving, "It's gone!"

"What's gone?" I ask, my anxiety at level ten.

"The notebook. Someone cut the soft top and broke in. Your car has trash in it, way more than usual anyway. The visor was down, no notebook, and your phone was smashed on the pavement." His face is a mix of horror and anger. I throw my hands over my face, reality creeping in. The second act of violence in a week. Aimed directly at me.

Before he's finished talking, Chandra is off the couch and out the door. Camera and cell phone in hand. She speaks quickly into her phone and snaps pictures when we catch up with her. She asks Brad what all he touched; he does his best to recall and point the areas out to her.

My beautiful car is a mess. The top sliced open in a jagged line. Resembling an angry sneer. A deep scratch, in a vicious wave, runs down the driver's side. The visor is hanging by a single screw, teetering in the morning breeze. Bags of rotten trash are thrown in the backseat, one has been torn to scatter the foul contents throughout the car. On the ground, next to the driver's door is a crushed cell phone. Far beyond cracked, it is smashed beyond repair.

A wail escapes from my lips. Who would do this? Who is this angry? And why are they angry with *me*?

Once again, our street is filled with police cars. Lights flashing and sirens screaming. I can't escape the sensation of having earned a target on my back. My whole-body trembles, an icy prickling sensation runs up and down my spine. The danger feels ominously close.

To add to the stress, Detective Cho steps from the car and strides directly toward me. Her expression is unreadable, but there is no sympathy emanating from her. Only a chilling sense of purpose. Any comfort the police vehicles had brought disappears. No wonder I felt danger looming. It's arrived in the form of a five-foot tall Korean woman. She is obviously on a war path.

"Hello, Mrs. Larkin. Shall I pretend that I'm surprised to see you again so soon?" Her clipped tone and stern expression reinforcing my anxiety. "Can we talk in the house?"

Brad gestures to the front porch and Detective Cho leads the way. Chandra follows quietly behind us, closing the door with an ominous click. We both know the trouble we're in. I can almost hear the hot water bubbling away. Into the pot we go, I guess.

"Cici!" The voice is like nails on a chalkboard. Nasal, sharp, and loud. Edna has arrived. I consider pretending I'm not awake. It's so early, 7:28 a.m. to be exact.

"I know you can see me on all those cameras. Now, answer the door!" She's clearly in a persistent mood this morning. To stall, I activate our doorbell cam. Edna is standing on the walkway. She looks fired up, arms crossed, frown deeper than the Grand Canyon, and her foot tapping furiously. Shockingly, she's still dressed in her housecoat and a pair of rubber garden clogs. I've never seen her when she's not put together and dressed for the day.

"Hey Edna, I can't right at this moment. I'm...indisposed," using a big word might give legitimacy.

She pauses for a second, almost considering if I'm telling the truth. She sighs loudly and makes a beeline for the door. Crappola! It hasn't worked and now I've poked the beast. Once on the porch, she leans into the camera and mouths, "NOW."

Groaning aloud, I drag myself from bed and into the hallway. My slippers make scraping noises on the wood floor, I'm literally dragging my feet as I schlump my way to the door. Swinging my arms, I resemble a child on the verge of a tantrum. I do feel a tantrum brewing. A big one. Edna's timing is as always, impeccable. Whipping the door open, I position myself in the middle of the doorway. Arms crossed, mirroring her angry frown.

"Yes, Edna. What do you need?" I growl instead of a hello.

"I have a bone to pick you," she begins.

"No doubt you do, but I cannot imagine what. It is 7:30 in the morning and I haven't left the house yet. How could I have angered you this morning?" I continue to match her posture and tone. She falters ever so slightly. The toe tapping stops.

"Well...I know...that," she sputters, emphasis on the last word. Exasperation replacing anger. "This is from the other day."

"And you need to come over here yelling first thing?" I cock an eyebrow and stare her down. I'm not in the mood for this.

"I certainly did, you will not get away with it again," she stabs a pointy finger in my direction.

"Get away with what?" I shriek. She's acting like I've attempted a bank heist.

"Parking in front of my house," she recrosses her arms, with a triumphant flair. A move that indicates she's won the argument.

"I'm sorry- did you say for parking in front of your house? When did that happen?" The last shred of patience I retained, has disappeared.

"I noticed the other day, when there were several cars. You moved your hideous truck in front of my house. In the process, you trampled flowers on my tree lawn," she proclaims. I nearly giggle over tree lawn, it is one of those New England expressions that pops up every now and then. But the outrage of her insult to our truck and stupid accusations take over any humor I find in the situation.

"Edna- are you seriously complaining that when LAW EN-FORCEMENT visited my home, I parked on the street?"

"They didn't look like any police officers I've seen," she sniffs, her chin pointing to the sky. It gives her persnickety appearance an even haughtier air. "I know what law enforcement looks like. My second husband was a detective, in case you've forgotten."

I pinch the bridge of my nose, suddenly feeling a gnarly headache forming. "Edna, what possible reason would I have for lying?" It comes out as more of a sigh than a sentence. I cannot take this today.

"No matter the reason, stay on your side of the street. You've caused more than your share of disruption to this neighborhood. Enough is enough," she says with finality, spinning on her heel and striding from my porch. Her clogs squeaking comically with each step. I'd laugh if I weren't so irritated.

I stare in disbelief, incapable of further response. Instead, I slam my front door with a force that knocks the wreath to the ground. I'll get that later. Retrieving it now will ruin the effect. It can rot in the sun for all care, right along with Edna's allegedly trampled flowers.

Chapter Eighteen

Chaotic Collateral

Frantic pounding at the front door breaks my concentration and I drop the measuring spoon into the mixing bowl with a soupy thwack. The batter splashes onto my face and neck. I gasp and blindly reach for a towel while shouting a muffled, "HANG ON!"

The dogs race me to the door. In the process, I trip on Coco and crash into the coat rack in the hallway, catching myself on the edge of the wall. This had better be super, super important. I can feel the bruise forming as I rush to the door.

I'm almost there and mostly cleaned up, when another round of pounding shouting begins.

"Cici!!!! Open the door!"

I cannot place the voice, but I fling the door open. It's Alfie, he has his hand up to pound again and nearly pops me in the head.

"Whoa! What is going on?" I call out, dodging his arm. He is stunned and disheveled. He appears to have run to my house. Sweat pours from his face, onto his shirt. He gasps for breath. My heart immediately sinks, is it Mirabel? Has something happened?

"Come with me! You have to come quickly!" he shouts and runs from my porch. I stare at his retreating back in shock for a few seconds. Sensing my hesitation, he repeats, "Come on!" with even more urgency.

Panic now rising in my chest, I push the dogs back inside and slam the door closed. As an afterthought, I press our electronic doorbell and yell, "Something has happened, Alfie came to get me." Then I bolt off the porch. The doorbell will ring into Brad's phone so at least he'll have some idea where I've gone. As usual, I have no idea where my cell phone is. New or not, I still can't keep track of the darn thing.

Running down the street after Alfie, my watch vibrates with a text from Brad-*be careful!*

Thank God for technology!

I spot Alfie turning between Mirabel and Geralds's houses. I try to take in as much as I can while following him. First of all, how is a man in his late sixties this much faster than I am? Focus Cici! Focus on your surroundings. I commit as much as I can to memory.

167

There is an unfamiliar car on the street. Alfie's shirt is soaked through and stained with a brown or dark red smudge. He has grass clippings clinging to both lower legs and is not wearing shoes. Odd that he isn't wearing shoes, what was he doing? FOCUS! I mentally prod myself. I doubt Alfie's bare feet are pivotal to whatever is happening.

We race into Gerald's backyard. Something feels wrong, what is it? My scalp tingles and a shiver of fear forms goosebumps down both arms.

The back door stands wide open, swaying slightly in the breeze. Gerald's beloved car is gone. One of the pots is knocked over, dirt scattered all over the back porch. I leap over it. Chandra's admonitions about scene preservation are in the back of my mind. Why? Do I think this is a crime scene?

We cross the threshold into the kitchen. Gerald's house is eerily quiet. A waving cat clock hangs on the kitchen wall. The cats bulging eyes add to the creepiness of the situation. Loud ticking emanates from another room, deeper in the house. The house feels stuffy and close, as if the air conditioning has been turned off for a day or so.

Before we can walk from the kitchen, Alfie stops me. Putting his hands on my shoulder, he spins me to face him. His breathing is ragged from the run, sweat trickles down the sides of his face. I notice his color is slightly off, pale with a faint gray cast. It gives him a waxy look. He is rank with anxious sweat. Whatever he's about to say cannot be good.

"Mija...I need you to stay calm," he says. Alfie's tone is serious and has a forced composure behind the words. I nod slowly while maintaining eye contact. My breathing feels like sips of air, coming in tiny gulps. I try to relax myself, but I've got a sickly feeling in my gut. Five minutes ago, I was attempting to make cookies, singing to the radio. With how quickly things have changed, I can't even imagine what the next five will hold.

Giving a sharp nod, Alfie releases me. We walk from the kitchen-he leads, and I follow. Silently, we walk through the house and up the stairs. Outside of a bedroom at the top of the stairs, we pause. The door is ajar, lights off, curtains closed. A fan whirs softly inside the room, rustling the curtains. That sickly feeling intensifies.

"Ready?" Alfie asks. I can't even react, instead I simply stare as he pushes the door open with the toe of his shoe.

"Noooo!" I shriek, covering my mouth as a wave of nausea hits. I rush into the room, but Alfie grabs me by the arm, halting my progress. He whispers a firm, "You can't."

Shaking free of Alfie, I creep into the room. To believe it, I need to see him better.

Gerald's body is bent in an unnatural position. His eyes are open, but he stares at nothing. They're glassy and unblinking. Dried foamy vomit had pooled around his head, creating a disturbing halo. His arms are twisted, his hands curled in tight claws. One leg is off the edge of the bed, the other tangled in the comforter. Something awful has happened to Gerald. Beyond awful. A foul stench emanates from the bed, a horrendous mix of vomit and human waste. The fan continues to blow rank air around the room. I put my hand over my face to block the smell.

Everything about this says he didn't die of natural causes. It's too grotesque to look at for long. Gagging and shuddering, I slowly back away from the bed.

"Have you called the police?" I whisper. My shaking hands fly to pat down the pockets of my shorts, searching for my cell. Disappointedly, I remember- I don't have it with me. In my haste to answer the door it was left behind.

"I did. When I found him. Then I came for you."

My eyes well with tears and I can't swallow past the boulder caught in my throat. Gerald didn't deserve this. He was a kind and generous man- taking care of family, community, and even strangers when needed. Things had been hard for him lately and we'd all tried to reach out. He assured us he was fine. Obviously, he wasn't.

"I don't understand what happened!" Alfie cries, disrupting my thoughts. The pain he's feeling must be immense.

"How did you find him?"

"We'd not heard from him in a couple of days. Elena made soup and asked me to deliver it this afternoon. Once I'd finished mowing the lawn, I came here. The door was open, which made me think perhaps he was injured or unwell. So, I came in. While searching for him, this is what I found," he stretches his hands out to take in the room in front of us. "I've watched enough movies to know not to go in or touch him before the police arrive."

In this awful moment, Alfie's final sentence strikes me as humorous. Despite the situation, I smile. What would we do without crime shows? Society wouldn't know how to act. Although, it might not be so good for criminals. They don't have that many secrets left.

"Good thinking! Your head is much clearer than mine would have been." I pat him on the forearm reassuringly and he clasps my hand in his. I'm not sure which of us is trembling more.

A faint wail tells of the approaching police and ambulance. This is happening too frequently on our street. Police shouldn't be here this often. The processor in my brain is stuttering. How can this have happened AGAIN? Our safe community has come under attack.

Alfie and I slowly descend the stairs, careful to touch nothing. I frantically try to recall any surfaces I may have touched on our way

171

in. The look on Alfie's face tells me that he may be thinking similarly. His eyes dart to railings, door handles, and light switches.

"Waiting outside will be better," I suggest. Alfie agrees silently, we make our way outside through the silent and stifling house.

Taking seats on the porch, we wait for the officers to arrive. Edna stands on her porch, arms crossed and a fierce scowl. She doesn't ask if Gerald is okay. Simply stares, angry, and unwavering. She's so helpful in stressful situations. Instead of the hand gesture I'd like to deliver, I throw a queen's wave in her direction. I see her stiffen, but still no response. Other neighbors have walked onto their porches, varying levels of concern on their faces.

With a start, I realize I never updated Brad. From my watch, I quickly tap out a message.

I'm okay. Police at Gerald's. Will call with deets.

He responds immediately with a thumbs up and then a heart emoji.

"We can't keep meeting like this," Sergeant Lawrence greets us, a tight smile on his face. Trying to make this feel less terrible. Failing, but trying. Mentally, I note him as one of the good ones. I'm glad he's come. And that Chandra has him in her corner. This mess would be worse without his guidance.

The officers and paramedics join us on the porch. We walk them through the house. I picture our procession as a morbid parade.

Rather than subject ourselves to seeing poor Gerald again, we decline to go with the team. From the base of the stairs, Alfie instructs the paramedics where to go. Sergeant Lawrence asks us to wait back outside and to have a seat until he returns. An officer stands near the door. The implication is clear, we are not free to leave.

Without my phone, I suddenly feel bereft. I ask the Sergeant if I can leave to grab the phone from home and turn off the oven. He agrees but asks another officer to accompany me. It gives me an icky feeling, as if I'm a felon planning to flee the crime scene. We walk in strained silence to my house. I'm thankful it is only two doors down.

What I didn't mention is that I have no idea where my phone is. This could take a while. It took hours to replace last week, and I swore I would keep track of it this time. Also- that I would not immediately crack the screen. At least I'm partially on track.

"I'll be just a moment," I tell the officer, lying through my teeth.

He nods politely and follows me in through the front door. Shoot, shoot, shoot. Now I'll have to search like a maniac in front of him. Not ideal. He takes a seat on the couch; I head for the kitchen. He cannot see the giant mess I made this afternoon. I won't survive the embarrassment.

The kitchen is an utter disaster. Instead of a peaceful baking session (which it was) it appears to be its own crime scene. Cabinet doors hang open, drawers gape, stacks of baking supplies are mounded on the counter. God only knows where my phone is in here. Frozen in place with indecision, I realize I have no choice but to fess up. There's no way he'll miss me frantically searching.

"If you spot a cell phone in a case with manatees on it, that one is mine," I call over my shoulder with a stupid looking grin on my face. I am trying to pass it off as a one-time situation, instead of the constant state of my life.

Oven off and a quick search of the counter and table. No phone. I distinctly recall reading the recipe on the shiny new screen earlier. Think! Where could it be? I check the fridge. That's gotten me before with car keys, no dice. Pantry cabinet, strike two. I am about to look in the dishwasher, when I hear, "Ma'am, I think I found it."

Entering the living room, the young officer is holding both dogs and my phone. He shimmies it back and forth in triumph.

"Thank goodness! You're a life saver," I gush and reach for the phone. Murmuring a few extra thank-yous as I tuck it in my shorts pocket.

"You remind me a lot of my sister and I tried to think of where she'd leave her phone. It was on the windowsill, behind the chair," a proud smile on his face. He clearly was the right person to send with me.

"I'd never have found that," I admit sheepishly. My cheeks burn from the stress.

"No worries, she loses her phone about a dozen times a week. We're all good at finding it now," he admits.

"We should go, huh?" I suggest pointing my thumb at the door. The officer places both dogs on the couch, giving each a small pat of the head. They sigh with contentment, these gals love company.

Once we're on the porch, I carefully lock the door. Leaning to have the officer in view of the camera. I make a phone call motion for Brad to see. A thumbs up emoji pops up in my messages. We walk down the few houses to Gerald's.

Alfie is still seated on the porch. Across the street, Edna and Hubert sit with the Avalons on their porch. Linda is with Desmond and the Cohens. All the neighbors seem to be interested.

Linda- *You, okay?*

Me-*No, something awful has happened to Gerald :(*

Linda-*He's dead, isn't he?*

Me- *Unfortunately. Alfie found him earlier.*

Linda- *It was that little twerpy cousin or whatever he is, I just know it.*

Me- *Police are inside now. No idea if they'll tell us anything.*

Linda- *Keep us updated.*

I dial Brad and give him the barest details, mindful that the police are listening to what I say or even don't say. Our friendly guard remains on duty, standing at attention in the open doorway. The fact that I am not crying has not escaped notice. Brad asks me to be careful and to think before I answer any questions. He offers to call his cousin Dennis, a lawyer in Miami, as a precaution. Seems like it may not be a bad idea. This day has gone off the rails, and I'm sure it is far from over. Promising to call me back with more info, he ends the call.

Before I tuck it away, another ding. Brad sending- *te amo muito* <3

Alfie is the opposite of me. He is full on crying when we arrive. Elena had called him when I was at the house. Talking with her seems to have unleashed his pent-up tears. She's on her way to Mirabel's now.

He tells me about meeting Gerald fifteen years ago. Gerald was married at the time, his wife, Marcy, died years ago. I nod, vaguely remembering her. He's been mostly alone since then. They had no children, and didn't seem to have family visit. That is until this alleged cousin arrived.

Alfie is now hiccupping from his tears, I offer him a tissue from my pocket. No idea how long it's been in there, but he doesn't seem to mind or even notice.

I share the story of meeting Gerald. His wife had recently passed away when we moved to the neighborhood. He was still grieving but welcomed us with open arms. Now that I think about it, I never recall family visiting either. The sadness of that hits like a tsunami. It's now my turn to cry. The tears flow in streams down my face. I lament only having a single tissue. Alfie tries to offer me a dry corner. I decline. That's a little too much sharing for me, even I have my limits.

Moshe approaches us with bottled water, a box of tissues, and a bowl of cut fruit. "Best I could do for now," he says by way of apology. We assure him that this is above and beyond. The sun is getting warm and we're both snotty messes. The provisions are exactly what we need to boost us up. We wave a thank-you to the group. Des and Linda wave back energetically, Francine waves but seems she's unsure why or who she's waving at.

A large white van with the Broward County Medical Examiner logo on the side pulls into the driveway. Two men get out. Standing next to the van, they pull white hazmat suits on and grab kits from the double doors. As they're finishing, a black SUV with the same logo drives up. A petite woman exits the vehicle. She's in a pantsuit and heels. Unlike the others, she doesn't put on the protective suit. She walks like she means business. We greet her with a "Hello" in unison as she steps onto the porch. Her scowling face turns pleasant. Almost like a light switching on. It seems genuine, which surprises me.

"Good afternoon, I'm Dr. Abi James from the Medical Examiner's office. May I go in?"

"Of course, please do. Most everyone will be upstairs," I respond. Why did I say it like there's a party inside? Good grief. She murmurs 'thank-you.' Before entering, she applies shoe covers and ties her hair back. The scowl has returned to her face. Voices inside call out, "Dr. James!" and "Welcome!" She's clearly liked by the team.

A short while later, Gerald is wheeled out. In a body bag. On a stretcher.

I am unprepared for the blow of seeing him leaving the house. It feels so final. The tears return, sobs shake my body. Next, the nausea. I rush to the edge of the porch and throw up in the bushes. Alfie comes to my side and holds my hair back.

"You'll be okay, Mija," he says softly, patting my back.

Chapter Nineteen

Questions but No Answers

Between my retching and sobs, I hear footsteps approaching and the soft closing of the front door.

"I know this is tough. No one sees this coming," Dr. James offers, she and Sergeant Lawrence have rejoined us. "Sergeant Lawrence will need to speak with you briefly, but you should be able to return home soon."

"She's right. If I can have a few moments alone with each of you, we can move things along and get you folks home," Sergeant Lawrence drops into the conversation. Without waiting for a response, he continues, "Alfie, I'd like to begin with you. Can you join me in the dining room?"

Alfie passes me, squeezing my shoulder for support. I clasp his hand and pat it. He'll be okay but entering the house holds extraordinarily little appeal to either of us. I know that I will never be able to unsee Gerald's glassy eyes and gaped mouth. Attempting to clear those last images, I shake my head. They're still there, a little softer now, but come unbidden the second I close my eyes. As much as I want to clear the scene in Gerald's room from my mind, I can't. The Police need to speak with me, and I'll have to relay it accurately. For now, I'll have to deal with it replaying over and over.

Brad's truck pulls up a few houses down with a screech, rocking back and forth as it comes to a stop. He must have raced here from the office. I shoot from my seat and wave my arms, mirroring ground crews at the airport.

"Brad! I'm here!" My voice cracks when I call his name, and the tears begin falling again. He jumps from his car and jogs toward me.

"Ma'am, you cannot have company right now," the officer advises. Despite the neutral tone, he wears a stern expression. I attempt to make eye contact, but his stereotypical mirrored sunglasses prevent me.

Turning back to the street, with a tearful, half-hearted shout, I tell my husband to wait. I hold up my cell phone and he nods briskly. Phone pressed aggressively to my face, I do the next best thing and call him.

Brad sounds frustrated and disappointed. His shoulders slump and he reluctantly agrees to wait at the Cohens. All I wanted was for him to run onto the porch and sweep me up in a hug. It would make this so much more manageable. Instead, I had to call and tell him to stay back. Adding another moment of pain to this afternoon. I scowl at the officer and fling myself into the chair furthest from him.

"You're up," the officer says abruptly. He indicates for me to proceed into the house. I hadn't seen Alfie leave. As I stand, I wonder if he's still in there or has been taken away by the police. Oh God- what if they arrested him? My spiral ends when I see Alfie shaking hands with the Sergeant and saying goodbye just inside the living room.

I sit in the offered dining chair and wait. I've also seen this on TV- don't start talking. You never know what will be taken from it, even when it's an officer you can trust. And I have a tendency to ramble, so it's especially dangerous.

"Thank you for your patience," Sergeant Lawrence says, grasping my hand in a firm handshake. His hand is about the size of a baseball mitt and completely envelopes mine. His notebook, pen, and a voice recorder are on the table. The young officer who walked me home is seated next to him. He introduces him as Officer Theo Delaney. "I'd like you to start with the beginning, I need to understand why you entered the home and what you discovered."

I pause momentarily, picturing Alfie beating on the door. It seems the best place to begin. I start telling about his arrival, opting to leave out distracting details (tripping on the dog, stumbling into the coat rack) and stop with our arrival to the house. For context, I share about the disheveled back porch. It was not Gerald's style to leave a mess. He was tidy to a fault. It was something I'd gently teased him about for years.

"Tell me exactly what you saw," he prompts. I describe the strange, musty smell and the claustrophobic feeling the house had. It seemed the house had been closed up for several days with no AC, how odd that seemed since he had family staying with him. Before I can move onto finding Gerald, the emotions roll in full force. My eyes burn and the familiar lump in my throat is back. Officer Delaney hands me a tissue and offers an encouraging smile. I take a second to wipe my tears, a few deep breaths and launch into finding his body.

"When Alfie pushed the door open, I was horrified. I rushed in to check on him. Alfie tried to stop me, but I couldn't help myself. There was no way Gerald was dead, I'd only seen him a few days ago," I continue, sniffling throughout. This was the first time I'd seen a dead body, and it was traumatic. Not to mention it was one of my friends.

"For the record, I need you to walk us through the entire time you were in the room. No detail is too small," Sergeant Lawrences says, prompting me to continue.

Over the last hour, I'd been forcing myself not to see Gerald, not to think about what I'd seen. The position of his body, the sights, and smells. Most horrifying was the vacant stare. My sniffles progress to a gagging sob. I can no longer sit still and bounce my legs up and down, attempting to calm myself. Reliving the shock of finding Gerald is too much for me.

"Please let me in! I can hear her crying. Please!" Brad's voice echoes into the house. His repeated shouts dissolve me completely and I crumple into the chair, sobbing loudly. With an irritated sigh, Sergeant Lawrence sends Officer Delaney to get him.

Brad rushes to me and wraps me in a tight hug. I lose all control of my emotions. Wracking sobs overtake me, I bawl into his shoulder. He rubs my back and tells me repeatedly, "You're okay." It does the trick, and I am soon calm enough to return to the retelling. Brad keeps a tight grip on my hand, our fingers laced together. His other arm protectively wrapped around me. With his encouragement, I continue.

"He was lying in the center of his bed, staring up at the ceiling. There was a horrible smell, like he'd vomited or something. I don't recall seeing blood or any weapons. It seemed like he died suddenly,"

I recount. My impression was that he'd been trying to get up or had been sleeping restlessly. I describe the angles of his arms and legs, how disheveled the bed was. Only his bedclothes were in disarray and the room was otherwise tidy. I'm not saying I've ever seen his bedroom, only that it matched his style with everything in its place.

I'm asked a few more rounds of questions, checking to see what else I can remember. But I am completely tapped out. My mind has turned into a black hole of nothingness.

Sergeant Lawrence snaps off the recorder, thanks me for sharing, and shakes hands again with both of us. We discuss the best way to contact him. He passes us a card and urges me to contact him if I think of anything else that may be relevant.

I ask if Gerald's family had been notified. The Sergeant looks at me briefly and tells me that Gerald had no family to contact. I'm shocked. Brad explains there has been a cousin staying here for the last few months, describing him and the extremely expensive car. We can't remember the name he gave us at the moment but promise to call when we do.

Walking back home, it pops into my head that Sergeant Lawrence should know about Gerald's company and the car. I'd given Chandra all the information I had and even sent pictures. It doesn't make sense. Distracted by this, I begin thinking out loud. I mutter to myself, "He should have known."

"He probably died in his sleep, babe," Brad says, still gently rubbing my back.

"Oh, sorry. I mean, Lawrence."

"What should he have known?" Brad is clearly confused. He's used to me starting mid-thought but in moments like these, he needs a little more context to catch up.

"About the cousin and the car. Chandra said she told him all about it and that he has the pictures," confusion turning into concern. "How did he have no clue what we were talking about?"

"With all that's happened today, maybe he forgot. Or he could have been playing dumb to see what we knew?"

"Could be..." I say slowly. "I need to talk to Chandra for sure."

Instead, I fall onto the couch and sleep for the next few hours.

Chapter Twenty

Big Movers, Big Losers

The next few weeks pass quietly. Honestly, I needed a break. Gerald's death knocked the wind right out of our sails. Out of all of us. For the first week, we looked as traumatized as we felt. Moving quietly through the neighborhood and about our lives.

Sitting on the porch, I watch the neighbors cross into the street rather than on the sidewalk right in front of Gerald's. None of us walk directly past his house since that awful afternoon.

Edna has paused her reign of terror temporarily, offering us a brief reprieve. We have a pool going for when she'll resume. So far Desmond and I are out, I didn't have much faith in her restraint. Moshe and Linda are still in the running.

This past weekend, we gathered as a community and hosted a fundraiser to pay for Gerald's funeral. His alleged family disappeared after his death and certainly didn't reappear during the funeral planning. None of us had a way to contact them and the police weren't able to turn up any details. We couldn't bear the thought of him having no funeral or memorial. As a group, we did our best to plan a service he'd have appreciated. I'd say that he loved, but that feels so wrong. How could you love your own funeral?

Despite having all of our planning complete, we're in a holding pattern. The police have ordered a full autopsy. There have been no updates on a timeline, so we wait. The police initially told us he'd died in his sleep, possibly a heart attack. But due to the circumstances, we wait for confirmation. It's a long wait.

Once again, I am struggling through a recipe- allegedly a simple carbonara, when my cell phone rings. Relief floods me, I can take a justifiable break from cooking. I quickly wipe my hands and answer, not even looking at the screen. Hindsight is 20/20, I most definitely should have looked.

"Cici," the shrill voice begins. It's Edna. I'm not sure how she's even gotten ahold of my number.

"Hi Edna! How are ya?" she's not going to dull my mood. I'll kill her with kindness.

"You've left the trashcans out again," she advises sternly. "This is the second time this month and I will not remind you again. I'll call the county next time," she threatens.

"Okay...thanks, I'll grab them in a bit. I'm cooking at the moment," I answer, still attempting to be patient. It's been a tough few weeks for us all. I'm not in the mood for a squabble or to listen to her monologue.

"Also, pull your car farther in the drive. The bumper is over the line of the sidewalk. The moving trucks are creating enough havoc without you adding to the mess," she tells me sharply then hangs up.

Hold up? Did she scold me and then hang up before I can answer? I block her number with more satisfaction than is probably appropriate. Returning to my recipe, it hits me- *she said moving trucks!* I shout it out loud to the dogs. They cock their heads to the side, invested, but also hoping for bacon.

I slide the back door open and listen. Banging and clanging, raised voices echo from the street. Absolutely the sounds of someone moving. My mind races with who it could be. Edna isn't the only nosy neighbor in this hood. Barefoot, I dash out into the driveway. Rushing as if the moving truck will peel out any second and disappear in a cloud of dust. At the end of the drive, I turn toward the noise. Sure enough, it's at Gerald's.

His house is being emptied by a crew. There have to be at least six guys carrying items out of the house and loading onto the truck. Who in the world would have approved this? A distant relative? Squatters? I watch for several minutes. Firstly, confused over what's happening. Secondly, they're so organized that it draws me in and I can't help but stare. It reminds me of those nature shows with ants carrying food to the colony. The spell breaks when the ramp is shoved into place with a horrendous metallic grind. Show is over for now.

Turning to go, Hubert and the Avalons walk past. He points at my cans and gestures toward the garage. I scowl and lift my shoeless feet one at a time, showing why I am not walking out into the road. My word, does Edna have them patrolling the neighborhood now? She needs to chill. Mrs. Avalon smirks and gives me an obnoxious finger wave. I'd like to give her a finger wave in return. Instead, I stick my tongue out after they've past.

I storm in the front door for a pair of shoes. Indignant that my neighbors are ganging up over the trash cans. I'm bent over muttering all the things I should say, would love to say to Edna and her nasty minions.

My phone rings somewhere in the house. Realizing the futility of the shoe hunt, I break off to search for it. Catching the call right before voicemail. This time, I take a second to see who's calling. Not getting trapped by Edna again. Relieved I see, it's Chandra.

"One sec, I need to grab shoes," I say, rummaging in the shoe cabinet. Why can I never find two that match?

"Okay, don't get the connection, but hurry up so you can listen," she says with a little snark in her voice.

"Long story, it involves Edna."

"Enough said," Chandra laughs out loud, "Get done with whatever she complained about. I'll talk while you hustle."

"I'm muting, you talk," I suggest, trying to be considerate. No one wants to hear trashcans dragging on pavement, least of all amplified through a cell phone. I don't even want to hear them.

"I set an alert for incoming theft reports. If one comes in that matches our cases, I get notified. There's been nothing for a few weeks. But guess what?" she doesn't wait for me to answer, "I got FOUR this morning!"

I'm sweaty from the heat and exertion. My sweaty hands fumble with unmuting the call. It takes far too long and I'm frustrated by the time I get it. I hear Chandra's muffled, "hello, did you hear me?"

"Shut up! Four? That must mean they're active again?" I whisper shout, my hand cupped over the mouth piece.

"You're being weirder than usual, where are you?"

"Driveway."

"Got it, with all those invested neighbors..." she trails off knowingly. It can rapidly change from peace to chaos here, and Edna always has ears in places they shouldn't be.

Yanking open the door to the lanai, I run and flop onto the chaise lounge. Looking like a teen in a nineties show- on my belly, legs kicking excitedly. All I need is a long phone cord and a bouncy ponytail. I pounce with rapid-fire questions. Trying to get as many details as possible. When? Where? Any recognizable names? Obvious connections? She fills in the gaps where she can. All have been in a five-mile radius, in the last seventy-two hours, no one we know, no connections stick out. She keeps the answers short and sweet. Which absolutely annihilates me, I NEED the details.

"Azúcar or my house?" I suggest, already shoving the dinner components into the fridge. Not sure why I ask, she'll want to see Seb if possible.

"Azúcar, give me thirty minutes?"

Exactly the answer I was hoping for! I hang up and dance into the kitchen. Picking up the dogs, we twirl our way down the hall. They're delighted to be involved with whatever is happening.

"Let's go meet Aunty Chandra!" I dress them up in summer bandanas and then scurry off to get myself ready. I'm in full cozy, house mode and need to get presentable in a hurry.

Chandra is seated on the patio when I arrive. The dogs parade through the cafe, reveling in the attention they're getting. Who doesn't love two smiley tiny dogs in flamingo bandanas? Seeing Chandra they give happy barks, pawing at her to be picked up. She scoops them into her lap and kisses their heads. It makes me smile to see them being loved by others.

A server deposits two coladas and two mineral waters on the table. I point and Chandra says, "I texted Seb that we were coming," beaming when she says his name.

"You're so cute. It's disgusting," I tease. She blushes and nods. Their relationship continues to blossom, and it is the sweetest thing to watch. I am absolutely thrilled for them.

"Okay, I'm embarrassed sufficiently. Can we order the rest and get down to business?" she presses the back of her hand to her flushed face, still smiling ear to ear.

I nod enthusiastically. Already picturing the fresh, warm pastries. Flaky crust, sweet filling. Right up my alley.

We order and then Chandra slides a file folder and notebook from her tote. She rests it on the table between us and smiles.

"Thought you may want to see these," she pats her hand on the folder, flips it open, and spins it to face me.

I crack my knuckles dramatically, bending my folded hands back for maximum effect, and grab for the folder. As I skim through the reports and notes Chandra has added, I start to see familiar phrases. All victims over the age of eighty, limited family involvement, officer taking report notes confusion or disorientation. I grab my own notebook to start jotting down thoughts and what I'd like to follow up on. There is nothing obvious at first, but I wonder if Desmond will know anyone on the list.

"I'd like to talk with them and see if they've got anything in common with my last group," I suggest. "I've got lunch with Desmond and Karen this week. Afterward, I'll go through the list with him." Chandra nods in approval. Desmond has become a big support. So many people open up to him, knowing he's a listening ear and a safe space. He ends up in the know for most of the community happenings.

"Pay attention to this one," she points to the third report, circling her finger on the date. I breathe in so sharply that I choke a little on my pastry. Recovering from near-death, I read through it more carefully.

"It's the day before Francine's wallet went missing," my interest is piqued.

"Keep reading. Take your time on the description," Chandra leans back in her chair, pleased with herself.

I quietly read aloud, "Mr. Edwards reports suspect was wearing jeans and shiny alligator loafers, noted and added to physical description." My mouth gapes open and I stare at Chandra.

"Told ya...you should see your face right now," she cackles loudly and smacks her palm on the edge of the table.

"Oh my word! It has to be the same guy," I re-read the description and can clearly see him. "How many Floridians are wearing dress shoes by the beach? Especially weird alligator ones."

"Yep! We've been trying to locate him too. Based on the article you provided; we went to the business. No luck there. Home address was a Chinese restaurant in Pompano. Employers claim he quit. We're still working on it," scowling, she picks at the edge of the folder.

"What if I tried? They won't expect me. I have nothing to do with the case from a legal side anyway," I propose. I feel Chandra's hand rest on mine, the weight of it distracts me from planning how I'd approach. I freeze and look down; this feels like an odd time for Chandra to become a touchy-feely friend.

"Stop drumming your dang nails, and think quietly," she flicks me lightly on the back of my hand.

"Thank God, I thought you'd gone soft on me," I snicker and tap my pen instead of my nails.

"Anyway, there's no way on this earth you're going near there. So go on and get it out of your head. This is part of an in-depth investigation. One that you are NOT involved in. Stay in your lane," she pierces me with an all-business look. I hold my right hand up, then place my left palm down on the folder. She rolls her eyes and gives a slow shake of her head. My antics aborted the speech I was about to get. Before she can begin again, Seb drags a chair up and plops into it. Throwing an arm around Chandra, he kisses her lightly on the forehead. She smiles with so much force, I'm concerned her lips will crack.

Seb catches up on what we've been talking about. I let Chandra share, not sure how much she talks about work with him. As expected, she gives an abridged version. I slide the folder off the table and into my bag while we talk. After a round of hugs and kisses for the pups, I take my leave. They'd rather spend time together, without me staring at them all goofy eyed.

Pulling into the drive, I notice the moving crew has finished. The truck has gone, and with its departure any of the personality remaining of Gerald's house. Depressingly dark and empty. The barren house too sad to look at for long. My mood has shifted from syrupy happiness for Chandra to gloomy over the loss of Gerald. I wonder how long it will be before a new resident moves in. How long before they feel like a part of the community?

All my joy from this afternoon has dissipated, I guess I'll go back to the dreaded dinner preparation. Fixing a coffee and walking the dogs may help return some of my good mood or at least give me a glimmer of motivation. Being outside always gets my mind right.

I intentionally avoid Gerald's house when we step outside. Making the turn toward Linda's seems like the obvious choice. She's waving from the porch as we approach.

"I've had a long day of appointments and could use a chat to decompress," she offers the dogs treats and for me to sit. I gladly accept. It feels like it's been too long since we got to have a relaxed porch chat.

Linda tells me of her morning of doctors' visits. She had breast cancer ten years ago and needs to have follow-up visits and testing. Today was nothing but good news and she received a clean bill of health. She rounded out the day with errands and lunch with ladies she worked with. All the gossip from lunch is shared with me and it gives me a twinge of nostalgia. Lunches with coworkers were about the only fun part of my job. Maybe it's time for me to start looking for work again? Is a weekly lunch filled with gabbing worth a commute? If that's the only draw, I can make something work around here.

"Did you see the new neighbors?" she asks, brow cocked up and suspicion in her tone.

"No! Give me all the details," I lean forward conspiratorially.

"Nothing confirmed, but they sure do remind me of that odd cousin of Gerald's," she huffs and glares at the empty house.

"How so?" my curiosity finds this tidbit irresistible.

"Other than dressing like they're private security, I can't quite put my finger on it. There was just something that seemed familiar," she taps her index finger against her chin, "too familiar for my taste." Nodding sternly.

This is news to me. The last I'd seen the house was empty and waiting for new occupants. There's no way that man is back, right? It wouldn't make sense. He fled and no one has been able to contact him or any other family for that matter.

The dogs and I continue on our little jaunt around the street. Stopping to say hello to the Cohens, they're off for a cruise with his brother and sister-in-law. I promise to keep an eye for them and Moshe gives me a spare key.

Having been gone for so long, we make our way back to finish dinner. I've frittered the day away and Brad will be home in an hour. Make or break time on dinner. As we walk, I quickly review the recipe and I decide it will not beat me. It's one of those recipe websites that caters to those of us who aren't skilled. I've pep talked myself into success. I cross into the house, looking forward to tackling dinner. An usual attitude for me, but I knew a walk would do the trick.

An hour later, I am plating the pasta and salad when Brad walks in. He drops his bag, and slides into the kitchen in his sock feet. I clap at his movie star impression and throw my arms around him. He kisses my neck with loud smooching sounds. Spinning me in a circle, he spies dinner and tells me he's starving.

Carrying the plates out to the table, he casually says, "Bentley is back."

Chapter Twenty-One

Saying Goodbye

Two days ago, we got the word that Gerald's body had been released to the crematorium. Despite his death remaining under investigation, his funeral can finally proceed. The services are scheduled for Thursday evening at Milman and Eberstein, a popular funeral home in the area. Most of the neighbors have prearrangements in place with them, so it was the obvious choice. Another facet of living in a community where nearly everyone is over the age of seventy-five, funeral home selection is commonly talked about.

Our little group gather at Mirabel's house the night before his funeral. We've decided to host our own celebration of his life. Mirabel and Desmond are taking this the hardest. They were closer to Gerald than the rest of us, having known him the longest. Each of us contribute something that was a favorite of his to make the evening less depressing. Desmond brings gin and tonics with limes from his backyard tree. Mirabel makes rice, beans, and plantains (Gerald was a vegetarian). Linda has a loaf of warm sourdough with homemade raspberry jam. Brad and I bring the one thing I made routinely for Gerald- individual key lime pie shooters with the graham crackers crumbled on top instead of a traditional pie.

Mirabel's yard is a haven. Lush plants, fragrant flowers, and twinkling lights throughout. On the back patio, we are seated around the large teak table. We eat and drink in his honor. Gerald was a special man who made room for his friends and neighbors. All of us share stories and memories, along with many, many tears. Desmond will do a reading at the funeral tomorrow, practicing with us reduces his nerves, and "gets rid of some of the tears," according to him. Over the years, they'd become more than neighbors and had a strong friendship.

He talks about the night Karen had her stroke. Gerald sitting with him all night at the hospital. Offering to drive him back and forth whenever needed, the meals and flowers he delivered. Gerald would visit Karen on his own as well, even after she was admitted to the nursing home. In fact, he'd gone with Desmond to tour the facility before her admission. With a voice choked with tears, Desmond admits, "I wasn't there for him the way I should have been. He's had those awful people staying with him. Instead of listening when he told me all was well, I should have gone over and insisted he let me in. I let him down."

Brad throws an arm around Desmond and lets him cry. There is no shame or embarrassment as most of us are crying with him. Gerald's death has created a void in our lives.

"Please don't feel that way!" I blubber out through my tears. Reaching over, I grab Desmond's hand in both of mine. "I tried, I called and called. Then I went over, thinking he'd let me in. He didn't. I even talked with him on the porch one evening. He promised me he was fine and would call if he needed anything. After that night, he wouldn't answer the door any time I stopped by. He would text me when I'd call to thank me."

Desmond squeezes my hand tightly as I talk, and some of the tension leaves his face. I am a teary, snotty mess when I finish and need to excuse myself momentarily. I go into the house to wash my face and attempt to calm down. That heaviness gnaws at my stomach, I can't bear to think of leaving Gerald with his cousin and whoever else was in the house.

On my return, the mood has lightened and everyone is smiling. Mirabel is sharing stories about game nights with her husband Manny, Gerald, and his wife Marcy. They played poker regularly. She brings out a spiral-bound, tattered notebook filled with game tallies going back more than a decade. We needed her humor to soothe us this evening.

In the back of my mind, the latest crime reports circle. This is not the time or place. I'll discuss them with Desmond another time. Tonight is for remembering our friend, not for adding stress.

Thursday is a dreary day, which does not help my mood. I'm feeling off-kilter from the emotions (and multiple gin and tonics) last night. It was a rough one to say the least. We stayed until midnight and then fell into bed the moment we were home. Brad was off to work early as usual, but he's rearranged his day to be home before the funeral. We're driving Linda and the Cohens. Desmond, Mirabel, Alfie, and Elena will ride together. No one wants to be alone this evening.

Two hundred people came and went through the calling hours and funeral service. Proof of the love felt for Gerald. It was wonderful to meet so many who were impacted by him or Marcy over the years. Dozens of former students and colleagues came by to share condolences and stories with us. He was so dear to them that many traveled in for the funeral. Over the course of several hours, many of us got to know a different side of Gerald. Oddly, none of his "family" were present. No sign of Mr. Cool and his fancy-schmancy car tonight.

Desmond did a beautiful reading from Psalms and Revelation. Sharing his desire to see Gerald again. Healthy and reunited with Marcy. He shared memories of their friendship and thoughts from others. It was a tear-jerker but so heartfelt and sweet. Truly the eulogy we all wish for- genuine, sharing the story of the life of a wonderful person. By the time he returned to his seat, there was not a dry eye in the place. Tonight was really an outpouring of love for our special neighbor and friend.

The car ride home is somber, each of us reflecting on the service and loss of Gerald. Little is said and no tears are shed. I'm feeling wrung out and thinking I need a few days to recover from the events of the week.

Turning onto our street, Linda inhales sharply and whispers a frantic, "Look!"

Following her outstretched hand, all of us look toward Gerald's house.

It's brightly lit, all the windows curtainless. Men carry boxes around inside the house. Several cars are lined up in the drive. Most notably, a shiny black Bentley. Loud music pounds from speakers somewhere within.

Passing the house slowly, we collectively stare in disgust.

Gerald's family has returned. Not to attend his funeral, but to take over his home while most of the neighborhood was away. Rage rises up into my chest, the fury delivering a crushing sensation. The strangers are staking their claim and don't care about appearances. It's like watching a dog pee on one of your precious possessions.

We drop off the Cohens, then Linda. Walking into the house, Brad heads straight for the dog leashes. I raise a brow with an unspoken question. He seems particularly motivated.

"Change your shoes and make sure to bring your phone. Chandra will definitely want an update," he says, a mischievous grin on his handsome face. My word, he's extra attractive when up to shenanigans.

I switch my shoes with lightning speed, and we dash out the door. Coco and Aggie are delighted to get another walk in. They run in front of us, eager to make their rounds. Brad encourages Aggie and me to walk in front. We normally walk side-by-side, but he urges me forward. He must have a plan.

"Honey, look this way!" he calls out, his baritone, bouncing off Mirabel's fence. I swing in his direction and see the phone raised. I get it now. Picking up Aggie, I say, "Smile for Papa!" She claps her tiny feet together and grins one of her cutest puppy smiles. He arranges his phone in different angles and passes Coco over to me. A mini photoshoot ensues.

Only once he says, "Beautiful! Got 'em just right," do we move on down the street.

To add more legitimacy, we take turns snapping photos all through our walk. We make sure each photo has a slightly different angle and captures as much background activity as possible.

Closing the door, Brad lets out a quiet whoop of excitement, pumping his fist in celebration.

"Let me see!" wiggling my fingers for him to hand it over.

"No way! I want to show you my favorite first," he easily holds the phone out of my reach. He scrolls at an agonizing pace, showing each photo from the end of the walk forward. I groan and roll my eyes, the urge to snatch his phone growing.

"Yes, yes, we are a lovely family. Now, can you pu-lease get to the good stuff!" I beg.

He sighs and says, "Fun killer," then swipes to the first set. I am in the foreground with Aggie. Behind me are the new neighbors. Faces as clear as can be. Once Coco joined us, he snapped a few more and then zoomed in; obscuring us from the photo. But the background. THE BACKGROUND.

Walking around the side of the house is none other than Stefan Markovic. I grab my phone to compare the newspaper photo to the one Brad has taken. It is the same man. I look up to see Brad's eyes twinkling and a big old smirk.

"Wonder what Chandra is up to right now?" he asks but I'm already calling her.

Chapter Twenty-Two

Lightning Strikes the Wrong House

B right and early (I'm more shocked than anyone), the pups and I head out to the lanai. To my delight when I woke up, the smell of brewing coffee greeted me. I swear it's what got me up. Last week, I finally figured out how to use the auto function on the coffee maker. We've only had it for two years, I was bound to learn at some point. Again, using my unemployed time to the fullest!

Brad was still snoozing, snoring softly with long puffs of breath. I let him stay in bed and took the dogs out to play in the yard. They were more than happy to have an early breakfast on the porch.

The day begins hot and humid. Just the way I like it. By mid-morning, Brad has joined us, and the temperature had risen to the low nineties. We're soaking it up, chatting about the possibility of an afternoon at the beach. Laying on the lanai, fan spinning like mad, iced coffee in my hand. Brad sips his hot coffee and reads. Aggie lays in the full sun, solar charging. Coco chooses a shady spot in the yard. I couldn't have been happier right now. Recent events have made me even more appreciative of quiet, peaceful moments with my little family.

My pondering is disrupted by the phone ringing. I send it to voicemail without checking the number. I've got another hour in my peace bubble. At noon, I am on deck to call Bingo at the community center. And I cannot wait. Spending a couple of hours with my friends will be the cherry on top. For now, I sit and sip. Ignoring everything but what's right in front of me.

"I-16!" I call into the microphone.

"BINGO!!" Desmond shouts, raising his card high in the air. Mr. Milton slaps his palm on the table, "Almost had ya!" he says good-naturedly. Desmond claps him on the back, grinning ear to ear. He's on a roll today and has won two of the games so far.

Glancing down the length of the table, Edna and Hubert are sneering. Neither make an attempt to be gracious at Desmond's success. Instead, they are talking and pointing, obviously gesturing in his direction. What could they possibly be mad about? Do they think there is some scheme, and Desmond has rigged the game? They seriously need to chill.

The next game begins, I call a series of combinations while other volunteers pass around snacks and beverages. Around ten minutes in, Edna rockets from her seat and bellows, "Bingo!" with the grace of a charging elephant. The crowd around her claps politely, without any of the celebratory zeal of the last two rounds. Hubert wins the next, followed by Mr. Milton, and another round by Edna. With that, our afternoon game comes to an end. Despite their wins, Edna and Hubert remain in foul moods.

In an event to keep some level of peace and inspire sportsmanship (is Bingo a sport?), I approach to congratulate each in turn.

"Hey y'all! Well done with the wins," I enthusiastically greet them.

"Humph... I thought you'd decided Desmond would win them all," Edna responds, dripping with derision. Oh geez, she's on one today.

"Nah! That's just the way the Bingo crumbles," I attempt a joke to break the tension. Hubert offers a little smile. On seeing Edna's sourpuss expression, he returns to scowling.

"It never seems that way when you call. Your little favorites certainly win a lot," she retorts. I haven't even come up with a response before she continues, "I've wasted enough time here today. I'm going on a cruise with my sister and need to go prepare."

Without saying goodbye, she strides away. Hubert in her wake. He still has some social skills and waves a goodbye, notably with his hand out of Edna's line of sight. The door slams closed behind them. All the others in the room snap their heads up. You can practically hear their eyes rolling. That woman is a menace, and no one is sad she's left.

Cleaning up after Bingo gives us all a chance to catch up over the last week. Desmond is visiting Karen right after and asks me if I'd like to accompany him. It's been several weeks since I've seen her, and I hastily agree. This also might be just the opening I've been searching for. We settle on meeting in an hour. If I get my act together, there should be time for me to pick up flowers for Karen *and* review the case reports. I want to be prepared when we chat.

Desmond pulls up front right on time. He's extremely punctual. I knew better than to be late. Tossing my notebook into my tote, I grab my fresh iced coffee and dart out the door. Sliding into the front seat, I present the bouquet of sunflowers and ivy.

"Aww...you know how to turn a man's head," he teases. I swat him with the bouquet and place it on the backseat. Thankful for the hardiness of the arrangement, a daintier one would have fallen apart.

"I have to admit- I've got an ulterior motive," Desmond shares. He's staring straight out the windshield, hands tightly gripping the wheel. I've not known him to be anxious before. In this moment, he seems unsure of what to say next.

"Whatever it is, I'm happy to help," I offer cautiously. Hoping that I am not digging a hole for myself.

"I don't know if you've heard yet or not. But there have been a few more robberies in the area," he begins. My mouth drops open, and I twist in the seat to stare at him. The silence must have concerned him, he sneaks a peek in my direction.

"You stole my thunder!" I exclaim and laugh with relief. So much for being stressed bring it up to him. He was way ahead of me. "How did you find out?"

"My group of golden oldies of course," a self-deprecating description. These folks are way more fun and active than they let on. "We met last week at the Pelican's Beak for breakfast. They'd clued me. I hope you don't mind, I went ahead and asked the folks to meet with you. Is that alright? I don't want to impose."

"It's better than alright! I'd brought notes with me today to ask if you knew anything about the new incidents. Do you think they'd be willing to meet with me and Chandra? After the last few weeks, I've learned some boundaries."

"I'm sure they will. Can you two meet with us this week?"

I immediately text Chandra. She's been anxiously waiting for an update while we dealt with Gerald's funeral. In seconds, she responds with fireworks-*YES!!!*

We go back and forth with a few dates for Desmond to take back to the group. The rest of the ride is spent comparing what Desmond knows to what is in the report. I take careful notes and am hunting for similarities. The biggest is the officer's voice. Similar to the last, this group describes it as whiny and nasal. It's so specific that it has to be connected somehow. There's no logical way it could be coincidental. We have the officer's name from the reports, but Sergeant Lawrence says his voice is neither whiny or nasal. Which is so odd. Each person I've spoken with describes the voice with the same tones. Could it be a voice he puts on when taking these calls?

Visiting with Karen is refreshing! Her progress is remarkable. She's now able to add a few words here and there to the conversation. Plus, her new lopsided grin is endearing and gives her a roguish look. When I tell her this, she claps her good hand on her leg and nods in agreement. Karen has always had such a sparkling sense of humor. It's such a blessing that it has carried on with her, despite all the changes. She's still there, only a little different now. The hope remains that she'll be able to come home in a few months.

We spent a couple of hours with Karen. Catching her up on all the drama and events. It was such a fun way to pass the afternoon.

On the way home, Desmond asked if he could take Brad and me to dinner tonight. Obviously, I accept before he's finished speaking. Spending an evening with Desmond will round out the day perfectly. Where to eat is an easy call, all three of us have a passion for spicy food. The local Thai place will send it through the roof. It's one of our favorites. Brad offers to drive since we've been out for the majority of the day- not that he hasn't but apparently, he doesn't care about his commute. I couldn't drive even if I wanted to, my car is in the shop. Still. Fixing the top is taking way longer than I'd expected. Which only adds to the continuing strain of it.

Thai Palace hit the spot! We shared three entrees, two appetizers, and soup. All spiced to perfection. We're riding the wave of exhilaration afterward. The one that insanely spicy food brings on. Back in the car, we begin making plans to organize a neighborhood party at the community center in the fall. Engrossed in calendars, Desmond and I aren't paying much attention as we enter the street. Brad's groan and the flashing strobe of police car lights jolts us back to reality.

"Oh no..." I sigh. Assuming the lights are somehow related to Brad and me. "What could it be now?" The house, my car, what's left that they can destroy?

"It's not our house babe," relief warms me with Brad's words. "Oh geez...the lights are in front of Edna's." The temporary calm replaced by a pang of anxiety.

"Edna's?" Desmond and I say in unison. He stretches forward, pinches, and pokes the back of my arm. His silliness breaking the growing tension.

We drive slowly up the street, taking in the multitude of cars and officers. Is she dead? Did she kill someone? Why are there SO many Cops? The new tenants of Gerald's house are notably absent, and the house once again appears vacant. Most of the other neighbors in our cul-de-sac are sitting on their front porch or standing in small groups. Linda waves us over when we exit the truck.

I half jog over to her. Brad goes to get the dogs. Desmond follows me but at a slower pace. I know waiting for him would be the polite thing to do. But I am far too antsy to wait a moment longer.

"She got robbed!" Linda whispers harshly, clutching at my forearm. I gasp and drop onto the loveseat next to her. Is it me or does Linda sound the teensiest bit happy about it?

Desmond plops into a chair next to us and leans in for details. Before she can begin the story, Brad rushes breathlessly onto the porch, a dog tucked under each arm. They wriggle away and make a beeline for Linda's lap. Once she has them settled, she excitedly launches into what's gone on this evening. She's practically levitating.

"About half an hour after you left, a police car came screeching down the street. Lights, sirens, the whole nine yards. Two officers jumped out and ran into Edna's without knocking. For a minute, I thought maybe she'd had a fall or something. Then the yelling started. She came out on to the porch, shouting at both officers. 'I am not addled! I know when something is missing from my own home!!' She was livid. I swear I could see her forehead vein bulging from here," Linda tells us. She speaks rapidly, still grabbing at my arm for emphasis. Clearly, she's more than a little keyed up.

"What was missing?" I ask, staring at the cars in the drive. By all of the fuss, it must have been a large or expensive item to warrant this response.

"From what I could overhear, she has a fireproof lock box that is kept in the hutch in her dining room. She and her sister Evelyn are going on a cruise. Edna went to get her passport, cash, and some jewelry from the box. It was gone! No trace of it. She swears it never leaves that spot. The last time she opened it was more than six months ago."

My eyes bulge. It tracks with most of the other robberies. Items that wouldn't be quickly noticed. Only two of the reports involved wallets. The rest were items that aren't routinely checked. A seldom used fire box of valuables is a prime target. Narrowing my eyes, I stare at Linda, "How exactly did you learn all of this?"

"It's Edna. She's been out here screaming and yelling for most of an hour. Anyone who comes within ten feet of her has gotten an earful. I thought pour Hubert was going to nod until his head fell off. He kept following her back and forth, listening and nodding the whole time," she chuckles between thoughts, "She called the police to report it. The officer taking the call implied maybe she'd forgotten. Edna went ballistic. Screaming that they'd better get to her house now. So here they are."

"Why are there so many cars?" Brad asks, astonished by the response.

"Well, as she often reminds anyone and everyone, her second husband was a deputy. After their divorce, he was promoted and promoted. When the officer gave her problems, she called him. Looks like he made a call. One car after another has come by. The crime scene team arrived not long ago."

In fascinated silence, we watch the subdued officers file out the house. A tall, silver haired man in a tailored suit brings up the rear of the parade. At the door, he leans down and stiffly kisses Edna on the check. She softens briefly, it may the most pleasant expression I've seen on her face. When he turns, she slams the door loudly. Officers cringe with the echo. Coco and Aggie begin howling and barking. Drawing unnecessary attention from the chagrined officers.

I turn to my porch buddies and see all three of their faces resemble mine. Mouth agape, eyes wide. Staring unabashedly.

"What the heck was that?" Brad says quietly. Shaking his head in surprise. "It was like watching a lion be tamed."

I giggle at the comparison. He nailed it. That man has some kind of special magic to calm Edna.

"Show's over! Get back in your houses!!" Edna's voice shrieks from her porch. She must have seen us all staring and cracked her door open far enough to screech at us. The whole neighborhood scatters.

Chapter
Twenty-Three

Toe to Toe

An irate Edna is a remarkable sight. By irate, I mean screaming, throwing things, bulging neck veins. She's unstoppable when on a tirade. This may (or may not, I don't really know) have contributed to her being married four times. Who am I to judge?

Edna is livid that her home has not only been robbed, but that she has been accused of being demented. We foolishly thought that last night was the grand hurrah. Surely enough officers arrived to make her feel she'd been taken seriously. Having the opportunity to berate a dozen or more is not extended to the general public. You'd think it would be out of her system by this morning. We severely underestimated her and the level of grudge she can hold.

The pups and I are out early for a walk and bopping along peacefully, when I think I hear my name. I'm wearing ear buds and listening to my latest mystery novel. So, I guess maybe I've misheard?

I glance around and don't see anyone on the street. Popping an ear bud out, I pause to listen. There's no sound initially and I assume I'd imagined my name being called. As I put the earbud back in, I hear it again, and there's no mistaking who it is.

"Graciella Larkin, I know you heard me!" Edna shrieks. I spin to the direction of the voice. She's in the side yard of her house. Gardening tools scattered around her. She must have been savagely attacking weeds in her flower beds. No idea how I missed the mess she'd created. It extends mid-way to the street.

"Sorry!" I lamely say and waggle an ear bud in her direction. The dogs utter low growls and Aggie kicks her feet, acting like a tiny bull about to launch at an opponent. I quiet them and walk in her direction.

"I'm sure you heard what happened?" she brusquely asks. I nod quickly, not wanting to add any fuel to her fire. "I blame you. It was you who brought all of this here."

Recoiling in surprise, I jerk my head away, yanking out my other ear bud. Backing up a few steps, I splutter, "What on earth do you mean?"

This is when the shouting and throwing things begins. To my horror, Edna picks up a clump of weeds and launches it my direction. Thankfully, her pitch isn't strong, and it lands with a plop at my feet. It seems to only make her angrier, she screams, "This is your doing!" and throws several more handfuls of weeds my way. Her next few throws have more oomph and strike me in the shins, the dirt crumbling into my shoes.

"Edna! That is enough!" I shout, "I am used to your insane behavior, but this is really too much. Chill out before you give yourself a stroke!" She stops throwing weeds but does not slow in her verbal tirade. The stroke comment seems to have amplified her anger. She's nearly purple with rage and sweating profusely. Unhinged is the only appropriate description.

"You can never leave things alone. You've brought criminals to our neighborhood. You and your friend, that girl cop. It's maddening! And now, I can't take my vacation. I should make you pay for it! Since you've ruined things."

"That's it! I'm done!!" I shout and storm away, ignoring the dirt squishing deeper and deeper into my sneakers. She's genuinely lost it. I think she may actually be having some sort of episode. In an attempt to calm down, I whip out my phone and call Brad. He suggests I call Chandra and give her a heads up. She might be able to help somehow. No idea how, but I am willing to give it a shot. This lunacy cannot continue.

Chandra is as horrified as I was. I'm shocked by how quickly she comes up with a solution. Rather than tell me, she simply says, "You'll see." The line goes quiet, and I realize she's ended the call. Is everyone in my life in a weird mood today?!? Geez. I stand, momentarily stunned, seriously considering getting back into bed and starting this day over later. Maybe by then the universe will have reset.

Before long, a shiny black SUV stops in front of Edna's house. I spot it out the window and can't resist the urge to go check out what the plan is. Fingers crossed that she's being arrested for harassing the neighborhood. That thought emboldens me to watch from the porch, instead of from my blinds in the living room. Snagging my topped off coffee, I settle onto a rocking chair on the porch.

Chandra is at the wheel. She exits with authority, striding confidently around the vehicle to the passenger door. She's in her full uniform, hair slicked back neatly into a bun at the nape of her neck- a hairstyle that says, "I'm not playing." Her gun belt squeaks a little as she walks to open the door. Craning my neck to see which power player is with her, I am nearly out of my chair when I spot her.

A petite Korean woman in a black pantsuit steps down onto the curb. Detective Cho has arrived. She and Chandra walk side-by-side to Edna's front door. As the door closes, Chandra flashes me a peace sign behind her back.

I am at a loss but nonetheless, one hundred percent invested in whatever is happening.

I sit on the porch and stare at the door with the intensity of watching a pot boil when you're starving. After a half hour or so, the front door opens. Detective Cho and Chandra exit. They shake hands curtly before leaving the porch. As they walk to the car, Edna gives me a death stare and shakes her head with an angry scowl. Her slamming front door echoes down the street.

The SUV takes off from the curb, in a sweeping motion, it turns in the cul-de-sac, and parks directly in front of my house. Is this some sort of remediation or has Edna convinced them to arrest me? Surely not, right? I stand and wipe my sweaty palms on my shorts. Gripping my coffee tightly, my hands shake a little. The coffee sloshes slightly. Embarrassed and anxious now, I sit the cup on a nearby plant stand. I don't want Detective Cho to see how nervous she makes me.

Chandra leads the way onto the porch, smiling broadly and makes a small "OK" sign with her right hand as she gestures with her left for Detective Cho to proceed. To my surprise, both are now smiling.

"Hi Cici, I'm pleased to see you again," Detective Cho extends her hand in my direction. I take it, shaking with her shockingly firm grip. Awareness dawns that I'm continuing to pump and staring, I break the handshake.

"Please come in..." I open the door, "Hope you don't mind dogs."

"Not at all, I have three," she walks in and drops to the floor. Allowing Coco and Aggie to kiss her face. Will wonders never cease...

"Coffee or tea? I'm on my fourth or fifth cup, but there's always room for more," I babble and meander into the kitchen. Chandra and Detective Cho follow me, each holding a wriggling and happy dog.

"Coffee for me, please. And call me Yoori," she responds pleasantly. The stern expression I'd seen on her face in previous encounters is gone, replaced by a happy and relaxed smile.

"I can do that! How do you take your coffee?" My internal voice is screaming right now. What the heck is happening? I slap a pleasant expression on my face, attempting to mask my unease.

"As black and bitter as my soul," her face returns to its stern expression. I mouth an "oh..." then recognize the mischievous twinkle in her eye.

"So, I'm guessing you want that iced too?" I suggest. She bursts out laughing.

"Nah, heavy on the cream and sugar, but piping hot," she giggles a response. Turns out I may like Yoori after all.

As if reading my mind, Chandra tells me in a singsong, "Told ya so..." I flash back to her telling me the rumors that Detective Cho isn't as bad as she seems.

I hip check her and murmur, "Heifer." Stealing one of her favorite digs.

Handing Yoori and Chandra mugs of coffee, I lean across the island and blink my eyes dramatically. "Assuming you have something to tell me?"

"You'd be correct," Chandra says between sips. "You got any snacks though?"

"Uh...is the sky blue?" She comes over to the fridge with me and begins selecting fruit, cheese, and leftover pie. As silly as it is, I love seeing my friends make themselves at home. I grab silverware and plates.

"Guessing this is an indoors conversation?" I ask. Hoping the answer is yes and that it is going to be juicy.

"For sure," Chandra says, her mouth stuffed with a bite of pie. "Did you make this?" she gestures with her fork.

"I did, is it gross?" eyebrows raised, waiting for her to spit it out. I eye the coconut custard with contempt.

"No way! It's stinking delicious. Might be better than the key lime," as she sticks another spoonful in her mouth. I wish I could pat myself on the back. Could it be that my cooking skills are finally improving? Instead of fishing for compliments, I do a little celebratory dance and scoop some onto Yoori's plate. Not even caring if she's a sweets person. I didn't need to worry, her high-pitched, "Mmmmm" tells me she is.

Pie devoured and coffee refilled, we move into the living room. It's like Yoori has had a personality transplant. Laughing, talking, relaxed back onto the couch with her heels kicked off. She and Chandra chat as if they've been friends for years. I don't try to dive into why they're here-when either are ready, they'll bring it up.

On the second round of refills, Chandra kicks off the conversation.

"Alright girly, let's get down to business," adjusting her posture and reaching for a leather bag she'd dropped by the door. Withdrawing a stack of file folders and a legal pad, she places them on the coffee table between us.

"I've filled Yoori in on what you've learned, and the info collected along the way, including your sneaky selfies," she says with a tight smile. I can't tell yet if this good or bad....

"I appreciate the effort you've put in and I'd like to apologize for our first meeting. Your concerns for your friend were not taken seriously. I am completely at fault," her eyes are downcast, hands resting tightly on her lap, and a slight flush on her cheeks. She seems genuinely upset. Clearing her throat, she continues, "After Chandra brought her notes to me, I realized how off track this has become."

Chandra opens the folders and reveals the organized contents within. Alphabetized reports and maps with areas highlighted. Another folder contains photos, and not just the ones I'd taken. Official police ones.

"We've used the materials you've given us and reports to get a better picture. The occurrences appear to be clustered. Pockets of thefts, none of them large scale. Until recently. The most significant is now Gerald's death. We heard from the ME's office; it is now officially a homicide. There was a lethal dose of Trazodone in his system. A medication that he is not prescribed, nor has he ever received. Evidence has been uncovered that now connects his death to the crimes locally."

My breath catches and my head spins. Gerald is the victim of a homicide. Hearing those words brings back all the memories of finding his body. Closing my eyes, I do my best to picture him in a different setting. Happy, smiling, spending time with friends at one of our cookouts. A few seconds pass before I feel collected enough to speak.

"May I?" Leaning forward, I bring one of the maps to me. It looks familiar and I try to focus. Jumping from my seat I grab my phone and zoom into the areas in my map app. Tapping my nails on the back of my phone, I go through the neighborhoods one by one. The silence in the room is thick, only the snoring dogs make noise.

Checking the final spot, I pop my head up, grinning triumphantly. Chandra's expression matches mine, "You got it?"

"Pretty sure," heart pounding, but not because I'm anxious. Rather more like vindication.

"I have a favor to ask," Yoori begins. I nod eagerly, not even caring what she asks. I'm in this far, there is not a chance I'd say no at this point. "Can you get ahold of all of your friends and friends of friends? I'd like to meet with them. There are some additional questions, and I believe they have the answers."

Continuing to nod, I dial Desmond's number. "I need help with something," I tell him after he greets me, "Can you come over? And maybe bring Linda too? It'll be all hands on deck." He readily agrees, no questions asked. Next, I text Brad.

Me- *Any chance you can come home early?*

Brad- *WHY?? Emergency?*

Brad- *Are the police there?*

Me- *Not an emergency. Chandra and Cho are here.*

Me- *She insists I call her Yoori. Pod people level.*

Brad- *No chance I am missing this.*

Brad- *Will take my next meeting from the truck. On my way.*

Brad- *Call if it gets too good.*

Troops assembled; I am ready to start planning. Desmond and Linda arrive, laden with snacks. Chandra immediately goes for Linda's macarons. Giving two to Yoori with a near breathless, "You gotta try these!" Dessert makes this woman borderline apoplectic. How she stays so fit is beyond me.

Using my notes and the contact lists in our phones, we get to work. Of the fifty-eight known cases, there are thirty-two that we can connect with directly. Sorting by gender, familiarity, and proximity, the list is split into thirds. None of us are interested or willing to call Edna. I know Brad won't be down for it either. She'll have to wait until last and I may send Chandra to talk with her.

Linda and I sit on the lanai, Desmond positions himself at the kitchen table. Chandra and Detective Cho (calling her Yoori all the time feels too weird) guard the snacks in the living room.

My first call is Tilly Ortiz. She was delightful and full of helpful information during our last few chats. Sadly, no answer. I leave a generic but brief message and hope she calls me back. Next up, I dial Eleanor Speer. While it rings, I hear Linda chatting with Alma Brittman, both seem happy to be catching up. Desmond is cracking jokes in the other room, he'd chosen to call Marvin first.

"Hello, Speer residence," a soft-spoken but strong voice. I remember it clearly.

"Hello Mrs. Speer, this is Cici Larkin," unsure if she'll recognize my name. Our last conversation was weeks ago.

"Oh yes! Hello, my dear," warmth added to her tone, I can almost hear her smile. "I'm so glad to hear from you." Relief washes over me, the next part no longer seems like such a big ask.

Directness feels like the best approach. I jump right in, "Would you be willing to come to our community center with some of the others and meet with a Detective? She has some additional questions and has asked if we could get everyone together."

"I'd be glad to. This is a chapter I'd appreciate closing off before I die," she says with a low chuckle. "I'll make arrangements for my caregiver, Adeline, to drive me. Can you give me the details?"

Ecstatic, I share the date, time, and address. She promises to be there and offers to pick up any of the others who may need rides. Ending the call, I do a triumphant shimmy in my chair, releasing some of my excitement and pent-up energy. Linda smiles and shakes her head. She tells me about her two successful calls, and I can see the pieces falling into place. This may actually work!

Brad comes home in time to help us finish. Instead of making calls, he compiles the list of those we've talked with and if they can join. Thank goodness he's highly organized; I'd have just used a sticky note or discarded piece of mail. My previous attempts at organization were discarded by a love of the quick access of paper. A spreadsheet is better and far easier to share than a handful of paper scraps.

By half past five, we'd spoken with thirty-one folks and have twenty-nine confirmed. Including the Cohens. Brad ran over between calls and spoke with Moshe. None of us have taken on speaking to Edna yet. Should we rock, paper, scissors to settle it?

Detective Cho is delighted with how many will be attending. She arranges for Chandra, and another officer to join and help with the interviews. Details are confirmed and we part ways for the evening. We'll meet back up in two days at the Community Center. Exiting the house, a demeanor change happens. Detective Cho returns to her stiff and stern persona.

Once everyone is gone, Brad turns to me and says, "Definitely pod people," a huge smile on his face. I burst out laughing. We've seen a completely different side of Yoori Cho. One that we actually like.

Chapter Twenty-Four

A Community Comes Together

A car horn blaring knocks me back to reality. I've stepped off the curb without looking and nearly walked into a shiny silver minivan. The harried woman at the wheel throws her hands up in frustration. I've got no excuse; I shrug and mouth *sorry* to her. Struggling with my bags, I step back onto the curb to let her pass. In a spirit of neighborly kindness, she flips me the bird and squeals her tires. Obviously, she's having a wonderful day.

I don't want to let her mood change mine. There is way too much to finish, I can't get distracted today. Hustling to the car, I load the bags and go over my extremely specific to-do list for the remainder of the morning. The meeting at the community center is this evening and I want it to go well. My emotions are in absolute disarray. Excitement. Apprehension. All to the point, that I am a whirling, wound-up mess. Time to chill out.

For a little self-care, I head to the drive-thru for a crispy, ice-cold Diet Coke. There is nothing like it on a ninety-five-degree day with eight thousand percent humidity. That first sip will erase any negativity in your day. Life altering, I promise.

Making the turn into our neighborhood, the momentous weight of the dinner tonight lands back on me. I puff out a hefty breath. Wishing that soda rush had lasted a little longer.

Today feels like an ending. I'm genuinely relieved to be turning the investigation over to Chandra and Yoori. After tonight, it will be off my plate, and I can move onto the next phase- looking for work. I'm not interested in returning to a job in the city. The plan for my future has shaped into coffee shop/bookstore/library type work. Something that will make me happy while providing some extra money each month.

The community center hits me with that icy blast of AC and I shiver with delight, reveling in it momentarily. What is it about that transition from blistering summer heat to arctic air? It gets me every time. Yet another reason I am all about summer.

Desmond and Linda are arranging chairs at a few round tables. We're trying to make it cohesive while also avoiding overcrowding. The goal is make the large room cozy and comfortable, all while providing space for private conversations. Spotting me, both rush over and grab bags of food and decorations. Despite the reason for the gathering, we decided it should also be a celebration. Detective Cho has not only taken notice, she's taking action. A triumph compared to where we were a few months ago.

"Cake make it safely?" Desmond asks me, concern evident over the lack of cake in my hands.

"Brad has offered to pick it up on his way, it was one less thing for me to risk dropping," I respond with a laugh and make a splatting motion, flipping my hand over quickly, palm toward the floor. I'm a dropper, always have been and likely always will be. Carrying a beautiful cake is not on my priority list. It would literally be throwing money away.

"Wise woman you are," Linda tells us, solemn expression conflicting with the mischief in her eyes.

Before we've finished setting up, Detective Cho, Corporal Amanda Davies, Chandra, and an unfamiliar female officer arrive. They troop in, all business. The three officers are in full uniform, an impressive sight. The youngest officer looks no more than eighteen but still commands quiet respect. She introduces herself as Miranda Fletcher. Detective Cho is dressed in her standard suit. Today it is a slim-fitting, deep eggplant suit with a tropical floral blouse. Black, pointed toe high heels clicking across the linoleum flooring as she walks toward us. Her outfit makes it obvious she's in charge and is here to make things happen. I grin at the four women with fierce intensity.

Chandra cocks an eyebrow as she approaches. "You smile any harder and you're gonna crack something," she teases, "May want to tone that down a notch or two." She then pokes me in the ribs with her elbow as a gesture of solidarity. Today may not be easy, but we're in it together.

Pushing the last chairs into the tables, we stand back to survey our setup. We're commending ourselves on how nicely the space has come together when the entry door bangs open so soundly, it cracks like a gunshot. En masse, we spin. I assume the wind has blown it open.

Nope. It's Edna and she is, as expected, in a foul mood. Face reddened, eyes bulging. Obviously angry, at what I'm not sure, but there's no doubt we're about to hear it.

"Well!" she bellows, "I'm here at your ridiculous party. Where is everyone?"

None of us speak. I glance at Desmond, Linda, and Chandra. The frowns and headshaking tell me I'm on my own. The thought of dealing with her makes my mouth dry, it's like I've eaten a handful of sand.

"Edna, you're early," I begin. Hating that my voice shakes. I swallow harshly and clear my throat to steady it.

"Of course I am. It's better to be early than late!" she continues shouting. Now she seems offended that I questioned her timing.

"Mrs. Sparks, would you care for a drink? We can chat once you're settled," Yoori interjects before I can whip out a hopefully snappy comeback.

Huffing, Edna crosses to the beverage station, hastily grabbing a bottle of water and aggressively shaking it in our direction. Yoori utters a barely audible sigh as she beckons for Amanda to join her. Escorting her to a table, they set up for the discussion. A small tape recorder is placed on the table between the three women. They each take out a notebook and pen, ready for action. It paints a picture of how seriously the conversations are being taken.

"To begin, I plan to record. This conversation will be retained as part of our investigation. Do you agree to a recording?" Detective Cho says in a clear, crisp voice. Her face a stern mask yet again.

"Of course I do. I wouldn't be here if I didn't want to have all of this investigated," Edna tartly responds.

My word, this woman is so genuinely unpleasant. Unlike the others, I am having a tough time feeling badly for her. There are times when what you put out comes back to you. Not that I'm saying she deserved to be robbed. But, karma. She'll getcha.

With the click of the recorder, Detective Cho announces their names and titles along with the date, time, and location. Edna is asked to state her first and last name and her agreement to be recorded. Housekeeping tasks are out of the way, Edna is asked to share her story.

For the first time, I'm able to see a vulnerable Edna, someone who needs help. We stay silent as this new version of her appears.

As she starts talking, the bravado fades. She takes a moment to collect herself. Her gaze falls to her folded hands resting in her lap. I notice then, she's holding them so tightly that her fingers have gone white. Sensing that she's being watched, she unclenches her hands and smooths the pleats of her skirt several times. With a long inhale and tight nod, Edna begins speaking.

"Our family has a love of cruises, particularly the Eastern Carribean. My sister, Evelyn, and I have been on dozens over the years. This trip was to be commemorative. Evelyn and Martin would have celebrated their fiftieth wedding anniversary next week. He passed away last year, and she has not done well since. It's been hard on all of us though, we've been friends since childhood. We'd hoped being together would make it easier on her," Edna dabs at the corners of her eyes with a tissue. "While packing for the trip, I discovered the theft."

"If you need a moment, you're welcome to take a break. We're ready to listen whenever you feel up to sharing," Yoori says soothingly.

Edna shakes her head and carries on. "I have lived in this house for three years. The day I unpacked, I placed my lockbox in the hutch. For decades, I've always kept it in the same drawer. Starting when my children were small, it was necessary to keep important papers out of their tiny hands." Children? Edna has children? I hear a whispered, "Well, I'll be..." from Linda.

"To my horror, it was gone. For a moment, I considered perhaps I'd taken it out already. But I ran through the last few days and realized I hadn't. There simply wasn't time to work on packing and preparing," her tone has taken on its typical perturbed quality. "I searched in any place that it could have been, closets, under beds, in the attic. It was nowhere. The more I searched, the more I noticed was out of place."

"Can you elaborate on what was out of place?" Amanda prompts.

"Well to start with, my silverware drawer. I have an antique set of silver from my great-aunt. The drawer was not fully closed, and the silverware was out of order. The napkin rings and two knives were missing. There's a method to proper storage and I follow it to a T," she sniffs when she says this. Reminds me of a stern housekeeper in a period drama. "I also found my jewelry case appeared to have been riffled through, although nothing was missing. I have the sense not to keep the good pieces in the house." Yoori and Amanda nod in unison while taking notes. Yoori pauses and looks over to Edna.

"Are you able to list what was inside the box? It may help with our recovery efforts.

"My family's important papers, most importantly my passport. I don't know if you've gone on a cruise before, but a passport is required. Without it, I cannot go," she stifles a sob with her cupped hand. Amanda passes the tissues across the table. Edna takes a few, offering a small smile as thanks. "I tried to get an emergency one. It wouldn't arrive in time. Poor Evelyn took it so well when I told her. Right in stride without missing a beat, she suggested we visit the Keys instead. Martin was a big Hemingway fan. She said he would have appreciated the trip." Tears cascade down her wrinkled cheeks, collecting along her jawline. "I let them both down."

I can't take anymore and start to walk toward her. Linda rests her hand on my forearm, giving me a cautioning look. Message received. This is not the time for me to be a softie and intervene.

Detective Cho gives Edna a moment while making a few notes. Once satisfied she's captured all her thoughts, she says, "I assure you, you've let no one down. This is an unexpected event outside of your control. Please do not lose sight of that."

Then she asks Edna to share her experience with the police department and reporting the missing lockbox. Her story is the same as dozens before with a twist at the end.

"The little pipsqueak I spoke to was disrespectful from the start," Edna's personality is returning and she is firing up. "When I gave him the details, he had the nerve to suggest I'd forgotten where I keep the items or had lent them to a friend. How would I lend a friend my lockbox filled with paperwork? It made zero sense. As I pushed the issue, he became increasingly dismissive. I cannot remember which of us ended the call. But I promised him they'd be hearing from Douglas."

By this point, we'd all become aware of precisely who Douglas was and the weight behind his name. An Undersheriff is far more effective than a run of the mill family member or friend. He intervened on her behalf. We'd witnessed the level of that action. Detective Cho has access to the report and photographs. She shares that no fingerprints other than Edna's had been recovered. The lock on the hutch had scratches, indicative of tampering.

"He had the most irritating voice as well. It was nasal and he whined throughout the call. Reminded me of a pesky neighbor boy when my sons were young. They really should reevaluate who is allowed to take those reports. I've already told Douglas that young man should be fired."

Yoori thanks her for sharing openly and promises to be in touch soon. Edna stands and walks straight toward our group.

A glimpse of a gentle and sensitive Edna hurts my heart. We spend so much time irritated with one another, I don't think of her as someone with emotions other than anger and bitterness. Imagining that I'm having a change of heart, I smile warmly at her. Walking past me, she presses her cane into the top of my foot and smirks. So much for that. I violently yank my foot from under the cane and glare at Edna. Chandra makes a *tsk-tsk* sound and rolls her eyes.

We reset the space after Edna leaves and finish shortly before our other visitors join the party. On arrival, Chandra and Miranda check their names and attach the appropriate police file in alphabetical order. We encourage all who come in to grab food and find a seat. Overall, it is a pleasant gathering. The tables are filled with lively chatter and laughter.

Once everyone has checked in, the groups split. Yoori and Chandra at one table; Amanda, and Miranda at another. This cuts the time in half. While they interview, I happily spend the time chatting with my neighbors and new friends. To my surprise, after talking with the officers, most stick around to continue visiting. It's easy to see how this has bonded them as a group, they've moved from isolated victims to friends.

By eight-thirty, everyone has gone but the six of us. Having limited interactions, I am not sure how much Yoori will share. I stay quiet as we clean up, hopeful that I'll learn something. Brad is taking out bags of trash while I bag the remainder. Bent and struggling with an overstuffed bag, I hear footsteps approaching

"I'm sure you want some details," Yoori says quietly. I jerk my head up from the trash bag I'm tying and nod aggressively, fairly sure I resemble a bobble head. We walk to one of the tables and she pulls out her notes.

In a matter-of-fact voice, she robotically recites the highlights. "Each of the instances has an officer who discredits the person making the report. The value of missing goods is below the $750 felony threshold. Few of the folks involved have family that regularly interacts. This leaves them vulnerable to predatory criminals and at risk of mistreatment. There is also a notable uptick in crimes in the area since Gerald's visitors arrived. All conversations point to organized thefts with potential involvement on a larger scale. We have some additional investigation to continue beyond this evening," at this, she closes her notebook and rises. I am struck by her honesty and all that she's chosen to share. I'm not law enforcement and was just helping my neighbors, I didn't expect to be granted the privilege of knowing the investigations progress.

"Thank you. Not only for sharing but for showing up tonight. It means a lot for this community to be heard and feel like they're being taken seriously," the temptation to hug Yoori arises but we do not have that relationship yet. Instead, I stick out my hand and she shakes it firmly.

Locking the door, I am filled with a sense of contentment. We did something good tonight and it makes me happy. Now, to get answers for everyone.

Chapter Twenty-Five

Cho Comes Knocking

Six days later, I'm out with Coco and Aggie for their doggie playdate day at "The Pack". They go to a play session with about twenty other dogs and run their little hearts out. In typical fashion, I didn't check the weather. Now, we're forced to rush if we want to beat the rain, jogging briskly along our street.

Two sleek black SUV's and three police cars glide past us. No lights, no sirens. It's weird how quietly they pass us. A tingle rushes down my back. Has something else happened?

Picking up the dogs, I break out into a full run toward home.

Eerily quiet, the entire neighborhood seems to have gone silent. Chaos is unfolding as we near the house. Police cars block the street, parked in a diamond, preventing entry by other vehicles. Officers bound from vehicles with weapons in hand, not making a sound. I only hear squeaking of equipment, heavy breathing, and doors softly closing. Realizing I can't make it past the line of cars, I divert over to the Cohens. Moshe sees me coming and waves me onto their porch.

"What is going on?" I squeak out, running up the stairs. Handing the dogs off to Moshe, I bend forward. Gasping for breath after my sprint down the street.

"I'm not entirely sure," he shakes his head. As he speaks, he rubs a hand up through his hair and then roughly down to his stubbly chin. "Francine is resting, today hasn't been a good day. I thought I'd read on the porch to relax..." he trails off.

"How'd that go for ya?" I tease. He chuckles softly and shakes his head again.

"Sit, sit," he gestures toward a loveseat on the porch. "We're going to be here for a while." The dogs and I plop down. Bringing my legs up, I cross them, giving a platform to rest my elbows. Leaning forward, I stare intently. I *really* want to take a few photos for Brad and Chandra. But that feels mildly inappropriate.

That is until I see Moshe with his phone raised, recording the scene. Shamelessly, I take my phone out and start snapping. With no explanation or context, I send them off.

Brad immediately responds- *stay where you are but keep me updated.* His next message is a meme of someone peeking out a window.

I promise to stay put at Moshe's and send more updates as things unfold. Right now, I don't have a clue what is happening.

Raising my eyes from my phone, I mutter an "Oh!" Detective Cho and two imposingly large officers are standing on Gerald's porch. Her sharp knocks echo down the street. She has the smallest hands I've seen on an adult, but doggone if her knock doesn't sound like gunshots.

The tallest of the officers' shouts in a booming voice, "This is the police! Open the door with your hands raised!" Despite the volume, the knocks and shouts are unanswered.

At the base of the stairs, an officer and a stunning Malinois are ready for action. The scene reminds me of a reality show. Unfortunately, the real thing is more stressful than exciting. I mean- it is exciting but WAY more tense than I'd imagined.

A clap of thunder coincides with the crash of the front door splitting from the frame. It shatters as the officer kicks through it. Detective Cho stands to the side as the others stream into and around the house. Shouts arise from inside, the K-9 officer and his partner crouch, ready to spring into action if needed. Coco and Aggie are on alert, their little bodies tightening to jump into the fray.

Aggie whines softly, Coco growls. I squeeze them against my sides, partly to calm them but mostly to prevent an escape.

Seconds after entry, there's a blinding flash of light accompanied by an explosive bang that rattles the windows. More shouting, it's unintelligible but sounds as if everyone is shouting at once. On the street, the radios squawk to life and the officers push forward to the house, guns drawn.

Moshe reaches out and grabs my forearm. We sit at the edge of our seats; the anticipation makes fifteen seconds seem like fifteen minutes. I hold my breath and try to be calm.

Two officers wrestle a young man out onto the porch. He kicks, screams, and thrashes. Making an unsuccessful attempt to halt their progress, he drops to his knees at the top of the stairs; nearly tumbling the trio onto the sidewalk. Another officer hoists him back to standing using the waist of his pants. With this, he roars like an animal caught in a trap and then gives in. Walking with the officers without further incident. I was so caught up watching that I missed the next man who is escorted out the door. He puts up no fight, instead he walks quietly with the officers. Gazing straight ahead, soundlessly, he descends the stairs in handcuffs. The men are placed in separate police cars.

A lightning strike of recognition hits, it's Mr. Bentley! The driver of the too fancy car. He's stoic and cold sitting in the back of the car.

The younger man is bent forward, sobbing. In a coordinated move, the vehicles turn in the cul-de-sac and speed away.

Moshe and I stare, mouths gaped, wide-eyed at one another. We resemble clowns mocking at horror. But this is legit, I am stunned by what we've witnessed. Sharing the unspoken fear that making noise will lead to being asked to go in the house, I mouth "Oh my God!" and Moshe nods his head dramatically.

The remaining officers stream in and out of the house, encircling it with crime scene tape. We hear an "all clear" announced over the radio of the closest officer. He's tall, rail thin, with mirrored shades in place. His posture tells all- he's holding the line. Even from this distance I can tell he means business. The softly pouring rain makes no difference to him.

A white van, emblazoned with the green and amber stripes of Broward County approaches the officer. Following a quick chat they're waved through to Gerald's driveway. As they pass, we see the "Crime Scene Unit" in bold red letters. I'd much rather see this van than the Medical Examiner version from a few months ago.

Hearing a gasp, we turn to see Linda step onto her porch. She stands with one hand over her mouth, and one clutching her chest. The drama of the scene clearly caught her off guard. I make a *PSSSSTTTTT* sound loudly. Whipping her head in our direction,

I hold up my phone and wiggle it. She takes the hint. Holding up her finger to give her a second, she retreats into the house.

Me- *police arrested two people!*

Linda- *this is what I get for napping :(*

Me- *don't walk around the front, cut through the yard, and come over*

Linda- *on my way!!*

Toting a bag of cookies and a mug of hot tea, Linda squeezes in next to me on the wicker loveseat and hands Moshe the bag. She leans in with her face over my shoulder.

"What in the world has happened?" she whispers. Her breath hot in my ear. Eyes glinting, she looks nearly rabid for information.

"I came up the street right after the police arrived. K-9's, big guns, the whole kit and caboodle. They KICKED the door in and then set off some kind of flash bomb. A young guy and Mr. Bentley were taken out of the house. The young one was screaming and wailing, good ole' Mr. B was stone cold silent," I whisper, my mouth centimeters from her ear. It took all I had not to shout. Pretty sure my hasty story has filled her ear with spit, but she seems unphased.

In response, Linda grabs my forearm in a vise-like grip, and mouths, "No way!!" She leans in and asks, "Where's Chandra?"

I shrug my shoulders and show her my text thread, the message with the photos hasn't been read yet. Her face is a mirror to mine, it's shocking that Chandra hasn't answered. As we stare at my phone, the message flips to read. It's almost like Chandra knows we're talking about her. Before reading her response, I stare at the group on the street. Has she been here all along and I missed her?

Chandra- *stay put*

Me- *lol...Brad said the same*

Chandra- *updates?*

Me- *two arrests- young guy and stone face*

Chandra- *thumbs up emoji*

Me- *you here?*

Chandra- *Nah. Catch up soon. Be safe.*

Me- *you too! Don't do anything I wouldn't*

Chandra- *too much room to work with...lol*

The next few witty texts go unanswered, and I am guessing she's back to work mode. I send Brad more photos and tell him to park at the community center and walk in. The street is still populated with vehicles, no sign of when it will clear up. He offers pizza and I accept, thankful I won't have to leave and make dinner. I ask him to get enough for the group. A thumbs-up and *ETA 35 min* appears on my phone.

I let Moshe and Linda know dinner is on the way, both grin in return and Moshe gets up to go into the house. He whispers, "Checking on Francy."

The clinking of beer bottles harkens his return. While I've never seen Linda drink a beer, she gleefully accepts the ice-cold amber bottle and takes a large swig. Following suit, I take a gulp of my own, the pups happily lick the condensation dripping from the bottle.

Brad texts- *parked and walking over :)*

Risking not being allowed back on the porch, I go through the side yard. Hoping I'll be less obvious than strolling down the steps. Brad has four pizzas, breadsticks, salad, and beer. I'd asked him to bring enough to share and he delivered. Walking as close as we can, I fill him in on what's gone down so far. He's so keyed up that he's nearly vibrating. It matches the rest of us. This is the wildest thing we've seen.

Taking seats back on the porch, we watch as boxes and bags are carried out to the white van. I lose count as a line of officers carry items out of the house. How much can those vans hold? My eyes barely leave Gerald's house as I stuff a slice of pizza in my mouth. Suddenly extremely grateful Brad brought so much. I am starving and sharing pizza with the dogs on my lap. They love the bits of crunchy crust and the melted cheese.

Footsteps in the house tell us Francine is awake, Moshe excuses himself. From inside we hear the murmurs of their quiet conversation. Francy joins us and is as delighted as we all are. You'd think at this point, police in the neighborhood wouldn't be a big deal. But this is, feels like closing a door on something. Not entirely sure what but something.

The van doors slam shut, and the driver pulls away. Another van takes its place and the parade of officers with boxes continues. Over the course of the next hour, it too is filled. By now, the street is mostly cleared, and dusk is approaching. Which in Florida, means mosquitos. The quiet smacking of us all fighting off the buzzy brats is an indicator; we need to head home.

Brad and I tuck sleepy puppies into our arms and say our good-byes. We decide to get together tomorrow and talk through the bizarre evening. I don't say it, but I sincerely hope I'll have some juicy information I can share from Chandra. My friendship with Yoori is too new to ask for any news.

With a massive soul-cleansing sigh, I fall backward onto the chaise on our lanai. Brad lifts my feet and slides in beside me. Despite the heat, he pulls me up close to him. Kissing the side of my face, he whispers, "Today was wild." I nod slowly, careful not to whack him in the face with the back of my head.

"Can you believe it? Last week, we were meeting at the community center with our friends to get them help. Now the cops are kicking down doors," I respond.

"Was that the coolest thing ever to see up close?" Brad asks excitedly. He loves to watch police shows and I'm sure he's sad to have missed most of the action.

"Yes..." I giggle. "It felt like we were in some reality TV episode. Kept waiting for dramatic intro music to kick up." Brad laughs at the picture I've created.

"In all seriousness, where were the news crews? Don't they usually show up to these kinds of things?" he asks.

"I'd have thought so too! But there was no one that I saw," reflecting on how odd it was. This makes it seem like it was some sort of secret operation. Sitting bolt upright, I smack my palm against Brad's thigh. "The newspaper clippings!" I shout and scrabble to get off the chaise. Remembering I'd given the original to Chandra, I grab my phone from the counter.

Brad has caught up with me by my return. "They're spread out all over south Florida...." he says, tapping his chin with his fingers.

"Yes!! When I talked with Chandra, she wouldn't tell me where she was. Do you think....?"I trail off, picturing the execution of a counties wide take down.

"Oh, it's happening. Wonder how many they'll get?" He paces back and forth on the lanai. Two little dogs at attention, following in his footsteps. "Can you find how many shops they have in the area?"

A search ensues, we collect all the store locations and then try to guess how many of the alleged family members could be involved. Totaling the numbers, I cautiously offer, "Maybe thirty?" Pondering the scope of who all might be part of the thefts; we are startled by the doorbell. I'm not crazy about unsolicited evening company, and stare at Brad. I debate not answering. He opens the app and shows me Chandra standing on the porch, holding up a bag of food. His face cracks into a wide smile, and he heads for the door.

Chandra practically collapses into the chair across from me. She's visibly exhausted. Her sleek bun has fallen out of place, make-up smeared, and a careworn expression. Before coming over, she'd changed into shorts and an LSU T-shirt.

"You okay, hun?" I ask, genuinely concerned. Chandra looks like she's been through it.

"It was a *long* day. Drove all over the place, hiding in spots, standing guard," she begins. I wait, knowing she's winding up and there will be more to come. "But we did it!" she exclaims. A beaming smile replaces her frown.

"Hold that thought!" Brad rushes in, he's been listening while plating the food Chandra brought. He has the meat, cheese and crackers piled on a large platter, surrounded by grapes and berries. In the other hand, a frosty pitcher of bourbon slush, cups tucked snugly in the crook of his arm. He tips toward me, and I grab the cups to pass out amongst us. "Proceed," he says with a melodramatic bow.

"You remember the newspaper article?" she asks, leaning forward to fill her drink. Brad and I glance at each other while nodding politely. Were we not just talking about this? "The 'family' in the article has shops all throughout this part of Florida. Surprising rates of petty thefts rise when each dry-cleaning shop opens. The incidents vary slightly across the state but there are commonalities. Enough to launch an investigation." A deliriously happy smile on her face as she pops cheese wrapped in prosciutto into her mouth. Taking her time to chew, she closes her eyes and rests the cold glass against her forehead.

A million questions are spinning around in my head, I try to snag one and make a coherent thought, instead I make a guttural spluttering sound. Similar to a caveman. Chandra laughs so hard that she coughs on her food.

"Seamless babe," Brad teases me. I toss a raspberry at him, only for it to be caught mid-air by Coco. We clap for her, and she does a little patty-cake clap in return. I scoop her up and give her a squeeze.

"I was trying to formulate one of my swirling thoughts into a question," I protest. "Now, do you think Gerald's visitors are all connected to the robberies?'

"At this time, I cannot speak to the involvement of those under active investigation," Chandra responds with a wink. Okay, well that is sort of an answer. I cock an eyebrow, staring at Chandra. Her PR style answer gave me a little motivation.

"How many people were arrested today?" I ask cautiously.

"In all of Florida? Geez that'll take me a day or more to get those results you," she replies with a smirk.

"You really came here to dangle a few details and have snacks?

"Of course I did. This is too much fun!"

I dramatically fling myself back onto the chaise, groaning "Why me?"

"I can maybe tell you what the next few days will be like?" she suggests as a peace offering. I rise like a mummy in a horror movie, arms stiff, gaze slack, and pivot to face her.

"You are a huge dork, but I'll share anyway" she laughs but then turns serious, "Arrests have been made in multiple cities and counties. Questioning has already begun. You may be called in to give a statement or to identify individuals," she pauses to let that sink in. I rub my hands together and do a shimmy in my seat. "Chill girl, this will be serious business. These folks are facing prison time for thefts and at a least a few for murder." Her suddenly sharp tone brings me back to the reality of the situation. I nod solemnly.

"When will she know?" Brad asks. I assume he means when I'll be needed.

"Within the next day or so. Detective Cho is leading the investigation now. It was reassigned to her after the meeting at the Community Center. She'll have someone reach out for you to come in."

"I'll go with you babe. Don't worry," he reassures me, knowing that underneath my excitement, anxiety is creeping in. I clutch his hand and give a weak smile.

"In others news," Chandra begins. Her voice is filled with sweetness and warmth. "Seb got a puppy!"

"No way!" Brad and I cheer at the same time.

"Can we do a playdate?" I ask, my hands in a pleading, prayer gesture.

"Oh, he's already asked," she replies with a giggle. "Want to see pictures?"

She passes her phone to us. On screen is a tiny brindled Staffy, a pink gingham bow on each ear. Her mouth is open in a wide grin. She looks thrilled to be held by Chandra and Seb. They're cuddling her between them, standing in front of the cafe.

"She is precious!" I exclaim.

"He named her Darla, which I find utterly ridiculous and cute," she says, still smiling. "Back home, I only know of dogs named things like Bear and Bandit. Never a Darla..."

We decide to have a beach date next week when Seb and Chandra are off work. I launch into playtime planning and give recommendations for classes and trainers. Chandra video called Seb so we could set up dates and see the adorable Darla. After disconnecting, she stands up to stretch and yawns loudly. I suggest that while this has been a fun evening, she should get home to rest. Brad and I walk her to the door, watching to make sure she's safely in her car. She drives away with a wave. I am suddenly overwhelmingly exhausted; this whole saga feels like it's nearing the end and I'm ready for it to be over.

Chapter Twenty-Six

Crumbling

Stefan Markovic sits in the interrogation room. His tear-swollen eyes and flushed cheeks contrast with his bravado. It's obviously an act; the poor boy is terrified. When he was booked, his actual age was discovered. Stefan turned nineteen two months ago. Barely out of childhood and here he sits, facing theft and murder charges. His citizenship has not yet been finalized, having moved from Serbia with his parents and twin sisters five years ago. The future his parents must have dreamt of is slipping away.

From the other side of the one-way mirror, I identify Stefan as the young man who bumped into Francine's cart at the grocery store. Cho thanks me for my time and turns to walk away. Expecting to be escorted out, I collect my purse and umbrella.

"You can stay, as long as you're quiet and don't distract the officers," Yoori offers. I nearly drop my purse from the shock, but instead I gulp down my enthusiasm and walk to the chair she's gesturing toward. Without further prompting, I sit quietly, legs crossed, attempting to project a demure and calm image. Meanwhile my insides resemble Jello in a blender.

Satisfied, she smiles brusquely and exits. The two remaining officers throw sideways glances at one another then return to their recording equipment with a shared shrug. I'm guessing this isn't her usual policy. Whatever the case...I cannot believe I get to stay. Unable to refrain, I do the tiniest of tiny happy dances in my chair, more of a wriggle than a dance. I'm too scared of being kicked out to do much more.

A door latches with a loud snicking sound through the speakers, heels click on linoleum, and Detective Cho enters the frame. The chair screeches as she pulls it out from the table. Taking her seat, she positions her notebook and pen in front of her, then smacks a file folder loudly onto the table. It booms through both rooms, startling Stefan and me. Clapping my hand over my mouth, I stifle my shocked squeal. Neither of the officers so much as flinch. This must be a more common occurrence than letting witnesses observe.

Silently, she opens the folder, flicking through a few pages. My anxiety is increasing by the second, pretty sure this isn't calming Stefan either. He's gone absolutely still- not blinking, shallow breathing, his fidgeting hands rest limply on the table. His formerly ruddy face has an ashen cast.

Yoori stops, crosses her hands on the folder and stares straight into his eyes.

Clearing her throat, she begins, "Tell me Stefan, did your parents travel round the world so you could become a murderer?" He doesn't respond, instead his face grows another shade paler (wouldn't have thought that was possible). "Was that their dream? To have a delinquent son? Shrouding them in shame for the rest of their lives?"

Yoori doubles down, "Mark my words, this will be the end of your time here. You will be returned to Serbia, with no chance of return. Not even for their funerals." He now shakes with fear, sweat runs down the sides of his face.

Tears fall from his eyes, and he cries out, "No!" Shaking his head violently back and forth, tears and sweat mingling and dripping onto the table. He collapses, bending forward to rest his face on the table. His sobs wrack his bony shoulders. Yoori lets this continue for a minute or so.

As his sobs wind down, she leans toward him. "Stefan, you need to listen to me carefully. Very, *very* carefully, "she says in a low tone, dropping her voice to a dangerous near whisper. It has the desired effect. He quiets and raises his head to look at Yoori.

"I need you to tell me what led to today. Not just you being arrested, but what you've been doing for the last several months, and why you killed Gerald."

Stefan sniffs loudly, his nose reddened, tears and snot dangling from the tip. Turning his face, he does his best to wipe it away on his county-issued jumpsuit. Yoori passes him a tissue; he bends to wipe his eyes and nose. Sitting up in his chair, he gives a determined nod. Decision made- he's going to talk.

"I came with my parents as a young teenager, we didn't have much money and things were, well are, very hard. My father was a professor at a private school in Novi Sad. My mother was a midwife. When we came to the US, they could not find work. Their English is not good, and they could not pass the tests they needed," he pauses to wipe his face as more tears fall. "I met some men at our church who ran local businesses and once I was old enough to work, I asked for a job." He sips from the paper cup of water on the table. It trembles in his handcuffed hands, water droplets shower onto him.

"Mr. Anton," he begins again, but Yoori interrupts, "Can you please share his full name?"

Curtly, Stefan nods, and states "Anton Dragovic." Yoori nods and scribbles notes on her paper, she gestures to continue. "Mr. Anton runs a lot of dry-cleaning and car detailing business. I started working at the dry cleaners in Miami when I was sixteen. At first, the work was good. It was the answer my family needed. I enjoyed learning how to use the machines and talking with the customers. It helped my English," he smiles weakly.

"After a few months, Mr. Anton began asking me a lot of questions about the customers, especially the older ones. He was interested in them sharing about vacations or visiting family. I thought he was trying to make friends with them, to get to know them. So, I would tell him about trips, special events, and errands. It took a few months before I knew it was more," he lowers his head, shame and embarrassment taking over. He reminds me of a forlorn child, about to be punished. His dejection is palpable and painful to witness.

"Can you tell me how it was more?" Yoori prompts, her voice is warm and reassuring, urging him to keep speaking.

"Once I started sharing with him, the customers would sometimes tell me about robberies or things missing from their homes. Some were sad, some were angry, some assumed they had misplaced it. There were too many to be an accident. Frightened, I went to Mr. Anton. In my mind, he could fix it. If an employee was stealing, he would find out who it was," he cries quietly, bending toward his cuffed hands, he dabs at his eyes.

"What happened when you told Mr. Anton?" Yoori quietly asks.

"He beat me," Stefan wails, the memory of that day filling him with pain. "He and two big men. He told me if I told anyone, he would kill my sisters," he chokes out between gasping sobs. "I had no choice but to work for him. I was told I'd been 'promoted' and would do whatever he told me to." Unable to talk further, he buries his face in his hands. Yoori passes more tissues his way and murmurs soft words of consolation.

Once he has calmed some, he snorts loudly and presses on, "It started with small things. Going into empty houses, opening cars left unlocked. I was not trusted to work alone the first few times, but when I had proven my skill, I was sent alone. I am not big, and do not frighten neighbors. I could walk around freely and be left alone." He smirks slightly while telling the last few sentences. It makes my skin crawl. Could it be that he's not as innocent as I'd assumed?

"When you collected items, where did you take them?" Yoori asks to move the story forward. She's trying to remain patient and pace the conversation.

"I was told it was time to move. Since I was almost an adult, my parents agreed. Plus, they needed the money. My promotion came with bigger paychecks, and they were afraid to lose them. When they asked what I was doing, I told them I was helping manage the store. They were so proud of me. I felt sick at my stomach for lying to them, but I could not risk the truth," the dejected posture returns, and he appears genuinely saddened.

"Tell me about the move," Yoori suggests.

"We moved to Fort Lauderdale to open the new store. He staffs his store with 'family' which are really immigrants with nowhere to turn. Loyalty is a given," he reddens, jaw tightening. "I was asked to work the front counter; my English is better than many of the others. In my conversations, the neighbors started sharing again. Vacations, funerals, illnesses, visits with family. All of it was passed onto Mr. Anton."

"When did the break-ins begin?"

"Within a few months of opening. Each store he opens, we follow the same plan. Befriend, then steal," shame radiates from him. "The people thought they were talking with a nice cashier, not a filthy criminal."

"How did the leftover items end up at the donation center?"

"I was told to get rid of it. We have boxes and boxes of stuff. The empty purses, wallets, and jewelry boxes need to go somewhere. It was a night that I felt heavy with guilt. My roommate drinks a lot and there is plenty of vodka around. I had several drinks, large ones, to make myself feel tough and drown my feelings. When the box was delivered, I remember thinking, 'Who cares if I get caught?' I didn't even try to think of a good place. I got on my bike and pedaled down the street. I saw a community center with an all-hours drop box, the lights were off and the lot was empty. I left it there- beside the other donations..." he trails off. Eyes glassy from the flood of emotions. He again bows his head.

"Were you hoping to be caught?"

"Not hoping, just no longer caring," he responds. Eyes still downcast, shredding little pieces from the damp tissue. That is until Yoori speaks.

"How did you go from guilt over stealing, to killing Mr. Phillips?"

"I didn't! I don't kill people!" he cries, terrified of her accusation.

"Mr. Gerald Phillips, you killed him and were living in his house until yesterday," Yoori's voice is ice-cold. Any trace of sympathy has gone. I slide to the edge of my seat, twisting my shirt into a tight knot.

"I didn't kill him!" he shouts again. "I didn't even steal from him. He was a nice man...." tears stream down his face and drip from his jaw onto the collar of his jumpsuit.

"Someone did and you were found in the house. Tell me who killed him if you didn't," she demands.

Summoning all his strength, he faces her head on. No tears, no sweat, only determination. In a calm clear voice he suggests, "Why don't you look in your own house for that answer?" Yoori stiffens and lays her pen down on the table.

"What do you mean, my own house?" she asks, voice tight.

He sneers at Yoori. His tone turns condescending, almost mocking, "How do you think we haven't been caught after all these years?"

With this question, one of the officers stands and takes a few steps toward me. Leaning down, he says, "Time for you to go." Before I can protest, my purse and umbrella are gathered up and he leads me to the door. Another officer outside takes over from there and walks me out of the building. Unsure of what has just happened, I stand in the rain staring at the building. The rain patters loudly on my umbrella and my sandals soak through. Cork does not do well in the rain. Realizing nothing will change by standing here, I climb into my Jeep and pull out of the lot.

On the way home, I try to call Chandra and Brad with no answer at either number. It occurs to me to ask Desmond or Linda if they recall chatting with the teenager at the dry cleaners. Desmond answers on the first ring.

Without introduction, I dive in with questions. He pauses, murmuring, "Let me think, let me think." Seconds go by and he exclaims, "Yes!! I tried a new dry cleaner around the time Karen was hospitalized. The front desk clerk was so friendly. I found myself chatting, probably told the poor kid way more than he wanted to know," he says with a chuckle. Desmond is a talker. I can easily picture him spilling too many details to Stefan.

"Can you remember what he looked like?" I hastily ask. I want to describe Stefan but don't want to sway him.

"Oh my, well he honestly didn't look old enough to work. Maybe he was fifteen or sixteen? Nice young fella," he again mumbles to "give me a sec."

"Do you remember any physical looks?" I prompt, my anxiety making me snippy.

"Slight guy, brown hair...that's about it. Nothing else comes to mind. He has an accent, sounded eastern European or Baltic? Reminded me of folks interviewed in a program I watched on TV."

I thank him, promising to catch up soon, and disconnect. Calling Linda next, I run through similar questions. As anticipated, she gives way more details.

"I do remember him! He was such a sweet boy, moved to Florida with his parents and twin sisters. He had the loveliest accent and I asked about his home country. If I'm correct, he's Serbian?" she responds. Leave it to Linda to find out so much about him in a few short conversations. This is just the proof I needed. Stefan was telling the truth, at least about the thefts.

It feels like I arrive home at warp speed. Screeching into the driveway, I run into the house. There's so much to write down before I forget. I fling my shoes and bag beside the door and rush to the kitchen. I'm desperate to capture all my thoughts on paper.

While I am frantically scribbling notes, Chandra calls. Knowing it will wreck my flow, but unable to resist, I answer.

"Hey super sleuth, what's up?"

"Oh nothing, just spent my afternoon listening to Yoori question Stefan," I say, trying to keep my voice casual and unhurried.

"Hold up...you what?" Chandra exclaims. "Never mind, I'm coming over. Get the coffee started." She hangs up and I sprint to the kitchen. Having no idea where she's coming from, it could be five minutes or an hour.

Ten minutes later, the doorbell chimes. Chandra's face appears, looking tense. Her response doesn't seem to match with what I'd told her on the phone, something is definitely amiss. The dogs dance and twirl as I unlock the door. Despite her strained expression, she bends to pick them up, planting kisses on their fuzzy heads.

"Well...howdy!" I chirp, trying to use a perky greeting to reduce the tension. Instead, she glowers at me and walks to the kitchen.

"Any reason why you're so stressed?" my chipper voice has gone tight, and my palms are starting to sweat. I swipe them on the sides of my shorts.

"Are you for real?" she snaps.

"I'm so confused. I didn't ask to be there if that's what you're stressed about..."

"Of course not! I don't care that you were there. It was great of Cho to have you listen in. You deserve that after all you've done to help us."

"Then what is it?"

"You don't know, do you?" Chandra appears genuinely surprised.

"Know, what?" I'm getting exasperated. She isn't giving me enough details to follow the conversation. What is so important that she isn't saying it outright.

"The connection to the department, you were there when Stefan brought it up," an exhaustion in her voice I haven't heard before. "He told Cho that there's someone helping cover up. I'm pretty sure I know who it is...."

"Oh my God! Who?" I shriek.

"I've been wracking my brain all afternoon and it comes down to one person," her face a mix of triumph and sadness.

Chapter
Twenty-Seven

All Falls Down

C handra stares down into her cooling coffee, swirling the mug rhythmically. She hasn't spoken in several minutes. Her breathing is tight and shallow, drawing an occasional sigh. Not peaceful sighs either, the 'I'm anxious and can't breathe' kind of sighs.

Her revelations this afternoon have deflated her; the triumph of yesterday is gone. Through a veil of angry tears, she shares her suspicions and the betrayal of trust.

"It's Sergeant Lawrence. In retrospect, it all makes sense," her hurt and anger raging. "He knew everything. I shared it all with him, including your involvement." My eyes widen, I wasn't aware how much she'd told him. "I took the evidence to him. Laid it all out, held nothing back. Our notes, suspicions, interviews..."

"Of course you did! He's your boss. What else were you supposed to do? You were doing what you thought was right!"

"Yeah, so much for that. How could I not have seen it? His abrupt behavior changes when I mentioned new evidence or connections between thefts. It all tracks," she laments. Her face crumples and tears shine in her eyes. "I didn't catch it though."

"You cannot beat yourself up over this. He's not worth it. Go out there, kick some butt, and make him pay his dues."

Eyes closed and a pouty face, she slides down to rest her head on the back of the couch and mutters, "Let me wallow for a little bit longer."

Then her phone rings, a delightfully, piercing fire alarm sound. She pops up like a jack-in-the box. Thrusting her mug in my direction, she struggles to get the phone from her back pocket.

"Boudreaux," she barks. Eyes bugging out, she gives a few quick uh-huhs followed by "Yes ma'am. See you in fifteen." She's on her feet and running to the front door. Slipping her feet into sandals, she says, "He's on the run. We're gonna get him!" I grab her bag and hand it to her as she runs out the door.

"Give me an update when you can!" I shout, but doubt she hears me over the roar of the Jeep's engine. Tires squealing, she blasts down the street. I'm calling Brad before she's to the stop sign. He's going to love this. Turning back to the house, I spot Edna and Hubert scowling in my direction. Fluttering a finger wave and winking at them, I jog up the steps. Edna's scoff echoes as the door slams shut.

An hour later, Brad bursts through the front door. "Any updates?" he yells, kicking off his shoes.

"Nothing yet," I say glumly. In a concerted effort to keep my mind off Chandra and Cho hunting for the missing Lawrence, I'd made dinner. Burgers (overcooked- I got distracted), baked potatoes, and corn on the cob. My notes from the last few months are scattered across the table.

"Dinner out back?" I offer, glancing at the messy papers.

In response, Brad opens the sliding doors and waves me to go first. Once we're seated, I run through what Chandra had shared and how it maps to timelines.

"It all started with the interview," Stefan told Cho 'Why don't you look in your own house for that answer?' when she questioned him about Gerald's death," I mumble around my ear of corn. Brad stops mid-bite and stares at me, mayo on his lip. I swipe it with a napkin and continue, "I was escorted out at that point. No discussion, just walked out by an officer." Gulping tea, I pause to get the timeline right.

"Chandra called me and told me she was on the way over. She acted like a complete weirdo when she got here. Was beating around the bush about why she insisted on coming here. I finally got it out of her, but it felt like forever," reflecting on our conversation, Chandra's tension and anxiety make my stomach hurt a little. She was visibly shaken by the afternoon. "Once she calmed down, she admitted there's corruption in the department and it points to Lawrence." Brad coughs on his food from the shock of her admission.

"Apparently, critical evidence in a few of the robberies has gone missing. Mostly digital stuff, specifically fingerprint result reports. There were other items on the log but not in evidence. No one had record of any of it being signed out."

"Like what?" Brad prompts.

"A few of the valuables, Chandra didn't specify. Crime scene photos were gone and records from reports were also deleted."

"Did he not realize computers have records? They can track who is looking at anything and certainly if you're dumb enough to delete records."

"Guess not. Seems like he panicked. Then went off the radar. Cho had been trying to contact him all afternoon. He's not answering his cell or at his house. Which doesn't help his case at all. When Chandra was here, she got THE call. The team is going after him."

"I wish we'd hear but it hasn't been long enough..." Brad laments, staring off into space. I drill my fingers on the tabletop, thinking back to my notes.

"Want to help me?" I ask, raised brows and a mischievous smile. We spring from the table and head to the kitchen. Coco and Aggie hot on our heels. Brad flips the tea kettle on to boil while I start explaining my notes and the timeline I've been building. Starting with the first robberies on report and moving to present, we map it on sheets of paper that we taped together in a long strip. We are nearing the end, backs cramping, eyes blurring. I check the clock, and it is well past midnight. Standing up to stretch, I pour more tea. My phone pings with an incoming text. Overstimulation and caffeine make me fumble while trying to open the lock screen. I look like a mime in a panic.

Chandra- *you up for breakfast around 8?*

Me- *ummm...yes!*

Chandra- *a lot to share :(Probably working the rest of the night*

Me- *dying for deets*

Chandra- *figured....lol*

Me- *our house or Azúcar?*

Chandra- *your house, not safe for public*

Oh man, this has got to be good! If we can't talk in public, she must be going to lay out all the details. Despite our renewed excitement, Brad and I call it a night. This has the same feel as right before a vacation. Emotions high and so much to say. Lying in bed we chat about our timelines until we both fall asleep.

Morning comes far too early. Brad takes one for the team and gets up with the dogs. I'm struggling to get my eyes open when he places a steaming coffee on my bedside table. Bending to kiss me, he whispers, "Wakey wakey."

I groan with the effort of reaching for the cup. Brad holds it beside my face and fans the delicious scent toward me. That does the trick and I'm able to crack my lids open.

"Hop to babes, Chandra will be here in half an hour."

As intended, this wakes me up fully. I fling the covers back and swing my legs over the edge of the bed. Wriggling my fingers toward the coffee, Brad places the mug in my hands and a kiss on my forehead.

The first sip is always magical. I can feel the caffeine moving through my blood. Brad murmurs "yep" and drinks loudly from his coffee.

"Blech! I gotta figure out breakfast..." my voice thick with sleep, it comes more as a croak.

"Taken care of!" Brad cheerily tells me. "I took some of the brioche out of the freezer and bacon. Figure I'll cook and you two chat. French toast, bacon, and eggs sound okay?"

"Way more than okay!" I throw my free arm around his waist and tuck my head into his neck.

"Get dressed and come help?" Brad asks, pulling me to my feet.

I text Chandra to come in when she gets here. Easier than having to answer the door mid-prep. She gives me a thumbs up and asks to make enough for an extra person. I assume she's bringing Seb. It's been a couple of weeks since we've seen him, a double breakfast date will be a nice way to catch up.

Brad flips the golden-brown slices of French toast while I hover over his shoulder. He makes perfect restaurant quality breakfasts and my mouth waters just watching. The same as the cafe, I am in awe. I dream of being at this level, but it doesn't seem realistic. Maybe I should take cooking classes? I can't get worse, so why not try?

A rapid double knock is followed by the front door swinging open. Chandra calls a quick "Hello" and I hear her shoes drop to the floor. Grabbing a slice of bacon, I slide across the floor toward the living room. Waving another piece of bacon like a ceremonial flag. At that moment, I remember I don't know exactly who she's bringing and wish I'd made a slightly more mature approach.

Chandra and Yoori stand on either side of the door. Loaded with bags and a change of clothes each.

"Moving in?" I tease.

"I should, I spend enough time here," Chandra retorts, thrusting a bag of warm bread and pastries in my direction. "Gift from Seb," she elaborates.

"Thank you for having us," Yoori says pleasantly. Her tone in contrast with her obvious exhaustion.

"Of course, please come in and make yourselves comfortable," I gesture toward the kitchen. "Brad has breakfast in progress and the coffee is piping hot." Chandra sniffs the air like a bloodhound and heads to the kitchen. Yoori and I follow.

"Would it be possible for me to change before we eat?" Yoori asks, holding up her clothes.

"A shower would be nice too," Chandra adds, sipping from her mug of coffee.

"That too," Yoori says and blushes slightly. As tough as she seems, she does embarrass easily. Or maybe she feels like she's imposing somehow.

"You got it! Right this way," I lead Yoori through our bedroom into the bathroom. Suddenly, I am very aware of our unmade bed and laundry spilling over the basket. "Sorry you have to tromp through here," I offer apologetically, "the guest bath is only a half."

"It's completely fine, we're here early in the day and I doubt you expected us to shower," she reassures me.

Returning to the kitchen, Chandra is happily munching on a slice of French toast and bacon. "Sample piece," she mumbles around a mouthful. I grin as she holds her mug out for a refill. Topping off all our coffees, I ask, "Guessing you'll want to wait until Yoori is back?"

"And until I've showered, I feel gross."

"Matches how you smell," Brad pipes up from the stove. At this, Chandra balls up a napkin and throws it at him. He grew up with three sisters and teases her whenever the chance arises. She is unbothered by him and seems to enjoy the rhythm of their friendship.

Yoori sighs loudly as she walks into the kitchen. She's been transformed from a professional to an average Floridian. Jeans, magenta tank, wet hair pulled into a bun. If I didn't know better, I'd think she was a local I'd see at the coffee shop.

Chandra snaps up her fresh clothes and makes a beeline for the shower, shouting, "Don't start without me!" over her shoulder.

Shaking her head and laughing softly, Yoori takes the coffee I offer her. While we wait, we chat. Yoori grew up on the Gulf Coast, along the famed 30A. Her grandparents moved to the area in the mid-fifties and the family has never left. "We wander but always come back," she says with a grin.

Clearly this is a recurring joke in her family, the retelling comes off as second nature.

"I've got eldest daughter syndrome. High achieving, work until burnout, bossy as all get out," she says and winks at me. "We come from a line of strong-willed people. On both sides of the family, so I come by it honestly. Most of the family has served in the military and are now in law enforcement. Our parents were in the Navy, which is partly why we've stayed along the coast." Yoori pauses to take a few sips of coffee. "My youngest sister is stationed in Hawaii, my middle sister at the Pentagon, the next to oldest is the Sheriff of Escambia County."

I'm impressed by how much Yoori is sharing about her family. Until now, she's been friendly and pleasant, but never talks about her personal life.

"Makes you wonder how I ended up here, huh?" she offers, leaning forward to grab a handful of blueberries.

"Kinda..." I say. It is surprising that she's here. I'm afraid of being offensive, so I don't ask. Why do her sisters have such big jobs, and she is here?

"Wait. For. Me!" Chandra shrieks from behind the closed bedroom door. She's fumbling with the handle and finally breaks out.

"Carry on!" she announces. Struggling to wrap a towel around her hair, one sock on and the other in her hand.

"Good grief," I stare at her wide-eyed. "We were waiting for you. No need to bolt out here half put together." Mocking a horrified face, I clutch at imaginary pearls.

"Okay then. Guess we can carry on now that we've got your permission," Yoori says with a smirk. "Anyway, I've lived on the east coast of Florida for several years. Following around assignments."

"Detectives get assigned to different departments?" Brad asks, puzzled at the thought. "I assumed you had to transfer to move."

"That's correct if you work for the Police Department," Yoori clarifies.

Chapter Twenty-Eight

Cleaning House

"**I** sn't that what you do?" I ask, starting to feel a tingle of suspicion.

"Well, I am assigned to departments but not a permanent member." Pausing to take another slow sip of coffee and adding more fruit to her plate. I can't tell if this for drama or maybe her exhaustion has kicked in and she's too tired to talk. Glancing up at us with a mischievous smirk, she finally says, "I am a member of a Corruption Task Force with the Florida Department of Law Enforcement. You may have heard it abbreviated to the F.D.L.E."

Mouth agape, I stare at Yoori. Brad inhales sharply and whispers, "No way!"

She's been undercover this whole time?!? It suddenly makes sense. Tough detective, no one likes her or knows much about her. Then the personality switch a few weeks ago once her suspicions started falling into place. All lines up but I am still shocked to the core.

"You mean to tell me- you KNEW? There was something going on and you were sent here?"

"Precisely that. The thefts have been reported for the last three years. My team was assigned to investigate two years ago. We determined it was connected to an officer locally. It was an officer who would have moved along the Florida coast. Heading south."

"How did you figure out it was Lawrence?" Brad asks. He's munching his way through a stack of crispy bacon. I can't hold off any longer and start doling out plates. Everyone takes the cue and loads up.

"Lots of watching and staff tracing. Who was where when the thefts occurred? It was always different desk officers, mostly rookies. Assigned to take calls and follow direction. They didn't ask questions," Yoori pauses to scoop eggs doused in hot sauce in her mouth. She makes a soft grunting noise and rocks side to side. I realize, again, she's our kind of people. Smiling, I stab into my tower of buttery French toast.

"Ten months ago, we concluded the perpetrator was someone in this department. I was sent in six months ago. Couldn't make friends, needed to keep my distance. It was key to keep everyone at arm's length. I could watch with objectivity. Hence the ice queen routine." The more she shares, the more it fits. There's no way she had a sudden personality change. She had begun to put pieces together and trusted Chandra, which extended to me.

"Within weeks, it was relatively easy to pin down who the perp was. Roger Lawrence began his career in Gainesville. He transferred to Daytona Beach in his thirties. Moving south every few years. By forty, he was a Corporal in West Palm Beach," coffee slurps as she gulps a mouthful. Brad refills her cup while she talks. None of us dare to interrupt. Chandra sits like the cat that ate the canary, fully wrapped up in the story. "Organized crime was making an appearance in pop-up spots. There were rumors of officer connections. Petty thefts, assaults, money laundering. But for the first year, it wasn't traced to anyone in particular." She refills her plate with eggs and more fruit.

"Back tracing showed his locations matched with a crime family from Serbia."

"Our neighbors!" I exclaim. Yoori smiles at me, like a teacher when you get the answer right. I get that same zip of excitement. It's starting to snap in place.

"You got it! Anton Dragovic, I believe you've been referring to him as 'Mr. Bentley'?" I smile sheepishly and she continues. "His family came from Serbia in the mid-eighties. From his early years, Dragovic was a problem. By sixteen, he'd been in and out of juvie multiple times. When he left home, right before his eighteenth birthday, his parents were relieved. At that point, he was involved with a larger organization. Some seriously bad dudes. His crimes escalated with his rank. He became untouchable. Any traction made during investigations would backslide into nothing. A low-ranking person always stepped forward to take the blame."

"Someone like Stefan?" I guess. Picturing him beaten into submission and fearing for his family, makes my heart ache for him. Strange to feel so much sympathy for a known criminal.

"Stefan is a classic example. Young man, employed by a semi-reputable company, then placed in a bad situation. It continues to compound over time. Crime on crime. To the point that they're in too deep to come forward. Until we get slip ups and anonymous tips."

By this point, we've eaten through every crumb of breakfast and carry our coffees out to the porch. Yoori tucks Aggie under her arm and sits in the rocker. Not to be outdone, Coco hops up into her lap. We sit around her, like kids at library story time. For several minutes, the only sound is the whirring of the fan and chirping birds while we digest what she's told us.

"How does Lawrence fit in?" Brad asks, he's antsy to find the connection.

"These criminals often target a shady officer. One with uncon-firmed accusations or suspicions of impropriety. Lawrence happens to fit that bill. Eight years ago, he was working on a money laun-dering case with a special task force. Seven thousand dollars went missing over a two-year period. It was taken in increments. Leading to all of the officers coming under suspicion. Unfortunately, there was no direct connection to any of the team. Each member was investigated, it turned up nothing- no large deposits, purchases or spendy vacations."

"You're killing me," I sigh and flop back on the chaise, hands thrown over my face. Unexpectedly, Yoori laughs, startling both dogs.

"Don't worry, you're almost caught up," she reassures me. "Roger left and moved further south. Heading into an investigative team in Miami. He didn't leave on a career high, there was still concern about the appropriateness of his behavior. Rather than stick to the straight and narrow, it appears he burrowed in deeper. There was an accusation of rough treatment of witnesses. Specifically, a witness to a crime involving Dragovic. This seems to have cemented their relationship. Again, a member of the 'family' stepped forward and confessed to the crime. The other reports in the case seemed to fade away."

"Until now..." Chandra chimes in, unable to restrain herself. "There were too many connections here. Plus, Stefan had no problem coming clean. He wants out."

"That he does. Lawrence and Dragovic picked the wrong location this time," Yoori raises her mug to Chandra. "There were too many to stay ahead of. Dragovic had too many shops in operation in the area. The crimes were happening faster than the goods could be processed. Mistakes were made. Roger tried to provide cover. Evidence has been deleted, gone missing from computers and property rooms. The vandalism at your home is another example."

"Wait- what do you mean by that?" Brad asks, leaning forward intently. I jump to sit up straight.

"We believe when I turned over our evidence, Lawrence tried to scare you off," Chandra admits. "The timing was spot on. Whether he committed the attack or requested it remains to be seen." I'm horrified that he would have attacked our home. It feels like a complete betrayal. I'd trusted him, even told folks how appreciative I was that he was on our side. Brad reaches and grabs my hands, squeezing tightly. He seems as unsettled as I am.

"But what about Gerald? Please tell me Lawrence didn't have anything to do with his death?" My concern growing by the second. The idea nauseates me, no doubt compounded by the gigantic breakfast I've eaten. The look passing between Yoori and Chandra does nothing to lessen my anxiety. Yoori quietly clears her throat, then crosses her legs and angles to face us directly.

"We believe that Gerald had served his purpose for Dragovic. At this time, we're unclear what that was. But it appears Lawrence was connected." At this, a sob escapes my lips. My chest aches, like I've been kicked. Brad grips me even tighter; his hand has gone clammy and his breath ragged. "His insistence on arriving at the crime scene with a selected group of officers is suspicious. On the exclusion fingerprint analysis, his were found on scene. Which is not abnormal, but several were smudged and the report showed they were older than the rest. There were additional prints on the back door and handrail. These appear to have been partially wiped away, rendering them useless. He did not follow procedure by allowing you and Alfie to stay on the porch together initially. He searched the house without another officer present."

"I was on duty and asked to come to the scene. He forbid it, told me that I was too close to the crime and it would impair my judgment. Which absolutely made sense in the moment. What was odd is that he instructed me not to text or call you, he said he would have you call me when it was appropriate. In retrospect, he didn't want me there or you talking to me while he was on scene," Chandra adds. Her face is tight with indignation. She pounds her fist on her knee as she recalls the day.

"I'd begun to suspect him after the vandalism. It didn't make sense. There were too many events from a single neighborhood, and it felt targeted. When I followed up with him, he said it was in hand. That one of his officers had a nosy friend poking around in local petty crimes, stirring up trouble. I decided to spend more time focusing on this side of the issue. You were the obvious choice for the nosy friend by the way," Yoori tells me with a snarky smile.

"Gee, thanks!" I murmur, feeling subdued by all I'm learning. Brad knocks my knee with his and smiles slightly. It reassures me a bit and I squeeze his hand three quick times. He returns the gesture; I relax and attempt to peel my shoulders down from my chin.

Yoori winks and continues, "The Medical Examiner, Dr. James, is a friend of mine and knew why I am assigned here. She gave me the lowdown after and told me 'the vibes were off' with Lawrence at Gerald's. I interviewed each of the officers on scene and did not find consistency in their reports. Indicator number one. Plus, the manner of death doesn't line up with Dragovic's previous crimes. An intentional overdose of a prescription medication, not prescribed to the victim speaks to someone who does not want to commit the murder in a violent way. As if they're attempting a kindness. It is also harder to trace. Evidence is rarer than in a shooting or stabbing death."

"Wouldn't we have seen Lawrence at the house?" I ask. The mental images flipping fast, blurring like pages in an album. I cannot picture him there.

"Likely, he would have been aware of your presence and gone to efforts to avoid you. Were there any times when a vehicle didn't match, or a driver stayed hidden?"

"The night of our stakeout!" Chandra and I shout in unison.

"Remember the black SUV? We never saw the driver," Chandra excitedly says. Nodding enthusiastically, recalling the destruction of my Jeep the following morning.

"He had to have seen us. And he obviously would have recognized you," I gesture toward Chandra. She grimaces and nods.

"Unfortunately, Gerald may have also begun to make connections," she adds.

"There were others in the department that were beginning to suspect Lawrence's involvement," Yoori tells us. I suddenly see Corporal Davies talking with Chandra, a small camera pinned to her uniform, pointedly avoiding specifics.

"Davies knew, didn't she?" I pick at my lower lip and replay the scene over and over. Trying to remember as much as possible.

"She had her suspicions and brought them to me," Yoori confirms.

"I wish I hadn't let Lawrence discourage me from talking with you. He assured me you were too busy and not to be bothered. He even promised he would discuss it with you at the next briefing," disgust thick in Chandra's voice. She scowls and grips her mug tightly.

"You were following chain, I would expect no less while in your probationary period," Yoori reassures her. "But now that you're through that, we have a little more flexibility." Chandra relaxes some and nods sharply.

"The event you held at the community center was our tipping point. We had enough evidence to proceed with arrests. From the Dragovic organization and for Roger Lawrence. You witnessed a small portion of those events. During the interviews, we confirmed much of our information. Stefan gave us a lot of what we needed. He even gave us names of others willing to talk. Anton Dragovic has maintained his silence."

"Where is Lawrence then? Were you able to arrest him as well?" Brad asks.

"Sadly no, he's in the wind. I believe some of the rookie officers he worked with tipped him off. Out of misplaced loyalty, they may have shared details he shouldn't have known. Which led to his flight."

"Any ideas where he's gone?" I nervously ask. The lanai has lost its sanctuary feel and now seems vulnerable.

"His boat is gone from the slip and his apartment appears to have been hastily packed. The important things are gone, passport, wallet, and a large cash withdrawal from his bank. Unsurprisingly, he left his cell phone behind. Lawrence knows we would use it to locate him," Yoori's voice is tight.

Chandra picks up the story, "we were out on the water for a good bit of the night. The Coast Guard picked up his location but lost him when he hit international waters."

"The current theory is that Lawrence is headed for the Carribean. Which island though is unknown at this point in time," Yoori turns her gaze to the yard. "I'll get him. Waiting is my specialty." She sits watching the breeze blow through the leaves of our large palm. Aggie licks her chin and breaks the spell. Yoori kisses the top of her head and Aggie wiggles in delight.

"He'll turn up," I say with forced confidence. Chandra shrugs and offers a half-hearted smile. My attempt at positivity falls flat. They've had long days followed by a long night.

"Lawrence may have gotten away, but Dragovic's organization is done for. Stefan has been fully cooperating. We'll only continue to learn more over the coming weeks," Yoori ends her sentence with a yawn so big, I can see her molars. She rests back in the chair, tipping her head against the cushions. Her exhaustion starting to overtake the triumph.

We all grow quiet, taking in the events of the last few days. My mind races and my fingers drum softly on the cushion beside me. Brad rests his hand softly over mine, then laces our fingers together. I squeeze his hand and sigh. The last few months have been a wild ride. Wrapping my mind around it will take more than just the morning. It's far from over...

Chapter Twenty-Nine

Property Values

J ogging past Desmond's, I throw a wave and smile. He eagerly waves back with one hand, saluting me with a mug of coffee in the other. Seeing the mug, I step up my pace. Coffee awaits me at home. Out of habit, I turn to check on Gerald's house. Despite the months that have passed, I still find myself looking for him in the neighborhood. He was such a gentle soul, and I miss him daily.

A shiny, large "FOR SALE" sign occupies the corner of the lawn. His house sits empty, no curtains or plants making it appear welcoming. The house has charm for sure with the wide porch and bright colors, I have no doubts it will sell. Who it will sell to is a point of frequent speculation. With each showing, we collect on porches to stare at the prospective buyers. Which, now that I think about it, is probably super creepy.

Mounting the steps, I swing the front door open. The dogs are frenzied with delight. Yipping and twirling while I peel off my sweaty shoes and socks. As time has passed, my nervousness has lessened, and I am back to feeling comfortable in our home. Locking the door once again feels optional, and the Fort Knox routine has gone by the wayside. I've never been great with routines anyway. One of the reasons we've loved this neighborhood since day one is the people. Watching our neighbors and friends pull together reinforced that for us. Thoughts of moving away have been pushed out of my mind.

Speaking of neighbors, Edna seems to have gone through some sort of transition. She and the cronies still march around, passing judgment. But now they are a slightly more friendly group. Stopping to say hello instead of shouting imaginary violations to rules of their making. Edna brought me cookies last week. Briefly I considered they may be dosed with laxatives. So, I shamelessly made Brad eat one first. He was willing to risk it for a crispy chocolate chip cookie.

The Avalons are even friendlier, they're hosting a backyard BBQ and have invited the whole street. We're actually looking forward to it. Which was a surprise to both of us. A positive from all the craziness is realizing we need to be more involved in each other's lives.

Spending so many hours working with Chandra and the crime victims inspired me. I'm done hanging around and reading. It's time to do something productive. I started volunteering with a victim hotline, offering support to neighbors in need. Secretly I've been looking at college courses online, no idea where that will take me. In the meantime, I'm starting work at Azúcar next week. Getting out of the house, spending time with people, and having access to free coffee sounds like an all-around win. Plus, I'll get to see Chandra consistently. She's at the cafe daily with Seb and Darla. If you listen hard enough, you can hear wedding bells in the distance.

We have cemented our friendship with Yoori, at this point, we may all be bonded for life. She was over for dinner this past weekend with her boyfriend and dogs. Who would have known the ice queen was really the karaoke queen? She's been a great addition to our friend circle. Her assignment here will be wrapping up in the next few months once the case goes to trial. We spend about half our time trying to convince her to move here. So far, no luck. But I'm nothing if not persistent.

Roger Lawrence is still actively under investigation. No one has seen or heard from him since the night he fled. Weekly more details about the depth of his involvement come to light. It keeps getting worse for him. If he's found, he'll spend the rest of his life in prison.

Anton Dragovic finally broke his silence, at the insistence of his legal team. The connection to Gerald was revealed. They only knew him through the dry-cleaning business. He'd talked about spending a few weeks traveling out west. A vacation we all knew about. He was so excited that he couldn't keep quiet. While chatting with the young crew, he shared too many details. Dragovic got word of the empty house. Once Gerald was safely out of town, Dragovic moved in. After ransacking the house and taking any valuable items, he made himself at home. Without his consent or knowledge of the extent, Gerald now had a rotating group of roommates. Threats of violence against himself and the neighbors kept him quiet. He was trapped by their presence in his home without saying a word. Fear does terrible things to a person.

Knowing the reason for Gerald's company brought some peace. None of us could reconcile his willingly hosting criminals. It didn't fit with who he was. But sacrificing his own safety to protect those he cares about certainly is. Gerald was a friend to most in the neighborhood, including Edna and Hubert. He helped me see that the true value of a neighborhood like this is not in the property, it's the people.

Pouring a gigantic, iced coffee and reading on the lanai sounds perfect right now. I need to figure out which dinner I'm up for attempting but that can wait. It's too early to depress myself.

Settling in on the chaise, I pick up my book and my phone dings.

Flipping it over, I see Chandra's name.

Her message? *Call me, I've got an idea ;)*

About the author

Kate Montgomery is a fiction writer based in Georgia, where she lives with her family and pets. A lover of dogs, coffee, and the beach, she finds joy in the simple pleasures of life. With a deep appreciation for the outdoors, Kate draws inspiration from nature, weaving themes of family, faith, and friendship into her stories. She believes in the power of words to build communities and create meaningful connections.

Other works by Kate:
"Southern Breeze & Mimosa Trees"

www.ingramcontent.com/pod-product-compliance
Lightning Source LLC
Chambersburg PA
CBHW010535100726
47903CB00011B/3016

* 9 7 9 8 9 9 9 8 6 4 9 2 1 9 *